DAUGHTER OF SHADOWS AND ASH

ARACELI'S BLADE
BOOK ONE

EMBER JOHNSON

CURSEBREAKER BOOKS

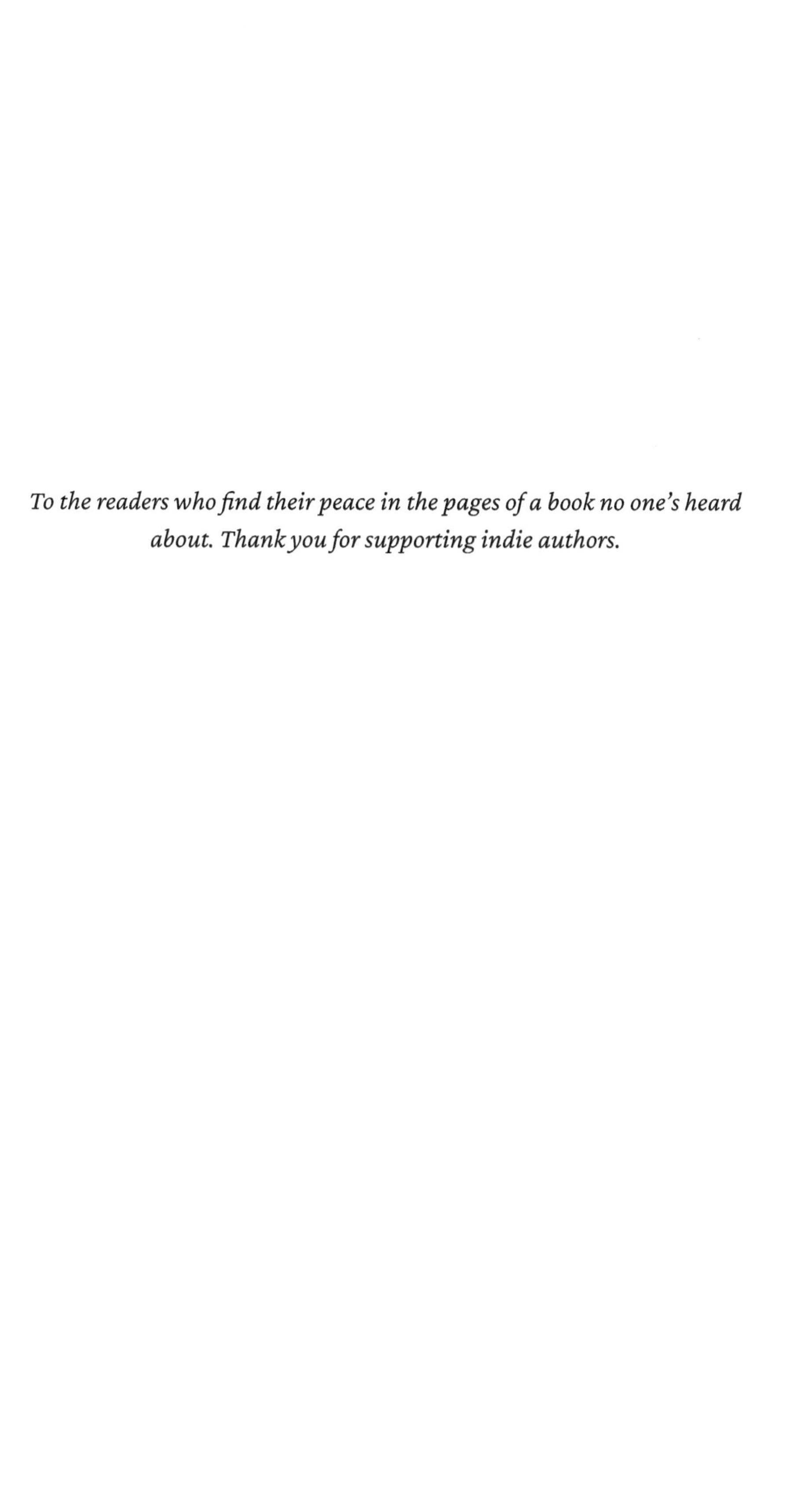

To the readers who find their peace in the pages of a book no one's heard about. Thank you for supporting indie authors.

To Téylie & Isla, the two greatest gifts ever bestowed upon me. You make life grand.

To Sam, I would simply be lost without your unwavering love.

PLAYLIST

IN NO PARTICULAR ORDER

Luminary - Joel Sunny
Ceilings - Lizzy McAlpine
Miserable Man - David Kushner
It Pours - Sabrina Jordan
DARKSIDE - Neoni
Running Up That Hill - Our Last Night
Blurry (Out of Place) - Crown The Empire
Ends of the Earth - Lord Huron
Hide Behind My Disguise - Cleffy
Daylight - David Kushner
You Found Me - Our Last Night
Work Song - Hozier
Higher - Sleep Token
Who's Afraid of Little Old Me? - Taylor Swift
The Night We Met - Lord Huron
Power Over Me - Dermot Kennedy
Iris - Our Last Night
000W000 - David Kushner
What Have I Done - Dermot Kennedy
Just Pretend - Bad Omens
Silence (feat. Khalid) [Illenium remix] - Marshmello
Middle of the Night (Violin) - Joel Sunny
Hold On - Chord Overstreet
Euclid - Sleep Token
Mouth of the Eden - Sabrina Jordan
No Place Like You - Thousand Below
Never Know - Bad Omens..
Love You To Death - Chord Overstreet
I Can do it with a broken heart - taylor swift
Meet you at the Graveyard - Cleffy

CONTENT WARNING

Daughter of Shadows and Ash may include the following graphic scenes and difficult topics intended for ages 18+. Please review before proceeding.

Death/murder, suggested rape/sexual assault, discussion of a plan to rape/sexually assault, deaths of loved ones, abandonment, torture, kidnapping, depression, grief, and other potentially sensitive topics.

ARACELI
THE LOST ISLES
THE WITCH'S COTTAGE
ESMERAY
Chermona
Oakston
Willowbrook
Souoak
Briarwood
THE GREAT WOODS
THE ASSASSIN'S GUILD
Bridgedale
Epherinia
SUNNEVA
N

CONTENTS

PROPHECY

When shadows lengthen and stars align, the weaver
of fate will tie the strings.
    Powers once separated shall intertwine, unleashing
power to shatter the world's very bones.
    The harbinger of flame and fate will save us all, a
beacon in the darkness a blade of all. Those who dare to
wield this power will rise, crowned in formidable glory.
    In the forge of blazing fate and destiny's weave, a
power beyond reckoning will awaken and cleave.
    For the merging of might that dances just beyond, a
siren's call of glory and bonds unbound.

CHAPTER 1

The forest held its breath, pierced only by the soft crunch of leaves beneath my feet as I crept past the massive trunk of an ancient redwood. The earthy scent of moss and decay filled my lungs, while shadows danced through the canopy high above, painting ethereal patterns on the forest floor.

I had been tracking a doe for the last couple of hours, hoping to bring home dinner for my grandmother and me. She had been my anchor, raising me since before my earliest memories formed.

My grandmother, Eleni, was gifted with water magic and a mysterious power that defied mortal understanding. Beneath her touch, water rippled with healing energy, and even the most stubborn wounds yielded to her will. Our gardens burst with life, overflowing with plants and herbs she used to create tonics for everyone in the village. The villagers looked to her as their guiding star, drawing comfort from her gentle presence, like moths to a healing flame. Our small community was a blend of fae, humans, and half breeds, bound together by something stronger than blood or magic. Her love nurtured all she touched, and Briarwood had her heart. The proof lay in the way wildflowers bloomed in winter beneath her windows, and how even the most bitter of feuds melted away at her kitchen table.

Lavender and moonflowers twined around our fence posts, their ethereal blooms pulsing with a soft, otherworldly light when darkness fell. The air in her garden always tasted of morning dew and starlight, even in the depths of summer, and visitors swore they could hear the plants singing on nights when the moon was full.

I watched her tend to Geralt, a man who had torn open his forearm with his own blade. Blood seeped steadily from the wound, tracing a crimson path along his skin. She guided him into our cottage's warmth while she gathered the herbs she needed. Her hands moved with fluid precision, plucking bottles from shelves without so much as a glance. The bottles seemed to leap into her grasp, familiar friends answering her call. Magic stirred in the air as she worked, heavy with ancient secrets. After grinding the herbs, she'd mix in a few drops of her moon-blessed water, then carefully paint it to the deep wound. Geralt closed his eyes, and my grandmother chanted in tones so soft they might have been mistaken for a breath. Her voice wove spells of comfort, drawing minds into peaceful darkness. I watched in silent awe as the flesh mended beneath her touch, leaving behind only the faintest silver line - a reminder that even magic couldn't completely erase the past.

At night, she'd tuck me into bed while whispering a blessing upon me. When I was younger, I'd ask her to tell me about my mother, and she'd smile sadly as she went on to tell me about some instance where my mother and her wild antics nearly brought her to an early grave. I never understood what happened to her. My grandmother always said, "She was lost." The hurt in her eyes made it difficult for me to press for more details. It was always an open wound, and it seemed easier to accept that she was gone as the years went on, buried somewhere in this beautiful land.

My father, I learned, was a guard newly stationed in a Sunnevan town bordering the woods. This scant detail was all my mother saw fit to share about my origins. From how my grandmother told the story, she sent my mother to the town to pick up some medicinal herbs she needed. My father laid eyes on my mother and instantly fell. They spent one fateful night together. My mother slipped out before first light, never to return to town. She confined herself to our little village until she had me and promptly vanished. At some point, I stopped asking my grandmother about her and vowed to right her daughter's wrongs by staying by her side.

I pressed on through the forest, grateful for the thin morning mist that allowed dappled sunlight to filter through the canopy. It would've made following the trail much more difficult. I heard the rustling of a bush to my left and swung my head around just in time to see my mark emerging into a clearing from the trees. A beautiful creature, unaware of the hunter that had marked its prey. I lifted my bow and took aim, sending a silent prayer of thanks to the gods, and released my arrow. The thwack of the bowstring wasn't enough to warn the creature of its fate. I watched the doe drop to the forest floor and began preparing to bring it home.

As I neared the edge of the dense tree line, Briarwood came into view. The laughter of village children and the bustle of daily life reached my ears, a welcome sound after the forest's silence.

I hauled the doe towards the butcher's shop, thankful it wasn't a full-grown buck. I wouldn't have been able to get it back on my own.

The door opened as I approached, "Late again," Geralt grumbled, stepping towards me. He grabbed the doe with his large hands and carried it into the back of his shop like it weighed nothing.

"I'm sorry," I called out. "Would half the meat buy your forgiveness? I may have gotten turned around on the way back."

Geralt reappeared by his counter and gave me a knowing smile, "You've lived here your entire life, it's amazing you still don't know your way around."

I rolled my eyes. "I know my way around perfectly well."

"You say that like you weren't asking Miss Betty where Anya's house was the other day when dropping off medicine," he chuckled. My face pinked with embarrassment. The village homes all looked so similar, and when you got turned around one too many times, it was almost impossible to remember whose was whose. "I'll take you up on your offer. Come back before supper, and I'll have it ready for ya."

I smiled my thanks and quickly left the shop. Since I had a bit of time, I made my way closer to the center of the village and found a quiet spot to relax. I pulled my bag to my side and reached in until I felt the familiar leather of my book. We didn't get many new books out here, being entirely dependent on what traders might come our way, but our general tradesman always remembered to bring something for me when he returned.

I took in my surroundings from my perch near the fountain, Maël stood with a small group of village girls, his easy charm on full display. Maël and I had grown up together, sharing twenty-one years of memories. Some days his lingering looks and gentle touches hinted at something deeper than friendship, only to vanish like it never existed.

Training alongside him and the other protectors had only cemented what my heart refused to accept.

We were friends—nothing more, nothing less.

Watching him with Lydia, a truly beautiful girl, made his indifference painfully clear. Her bell-like laughter floated across the square as she traced her fingers along his arm, drawing out that sun-bright smile I coveted.

I forced my gaze back to the pages before me, ignoring the bitter taste of jealousy on my tongue. They would make a perfect match— the kind written in songs—and I hated how much that truth carved at my heart.

I had just found my place in the story when a familiar hand darted into view, stealing away my escape.

"What saucy things are you reading today, hmm?" The deep timbre of his voice sent shivers down my spine. I looked up to see

Maël standing over me, a playful smile across his stupidly handsome face. I glared up at him and jumped to my feet, my arm extended in an attempt to recover my book, frustrated as he held it just out of my grasp. Despite being full fae, he towered over me. What good was being a "magical" being if all you had to show for it were pointed ears and fangs.

"Just learning how to gut you in your sleep," I huffed.

"That doesn't sound very pleasant," he laughed. His brown eyes gleamed with gold as a smile crept across his face. "I have a bargain for you, if you're interested, that is." He glanced at the page I had opened to, shaking his head at whatever smut he must've come across.

I took a step back and crossed my arms, "I'm not interested in making bargains with demons."

He feigned hurt, holding the book to his chest as if I've stabbed him there. "I'm hurt, Lor. I thought we were better friends than that."

"Friends don't steal portals to other worlds from friends."

He scrunched his face. "It's a book, not a portal. I see you came out of the woods grumpy today."

Maël handed my book back, and I hugged it to my chest.

"Books transport you to places you could never go to otherwise. How did you know I was just in the woods? Following me around like a lost dog is unbecoming of you."

"First I'm a demon, now I'm a dog. Tomorrow, I'm afraid you'll say I'm a pig."

I smirked and looked up at him through thick lashes, "Tomorrow has yet to be seen."

"I saw you come from Geralt's, and you've got leaves in your hair still." He picked one of the offending leaves from the top of my head and crumbled it in his large hand.

"Ah," heat crept up my neck as I frantically combed through my dark hair for any remaining leaves.

"You're welcome. I'm headed to the training grounds. Come find me later. And if you feel like getting your ass kicked, you know where to find me."

He flashed that infuriating smirk of his and walked away.

Sometimes I wondered if he knew exactly how maddening he was. I let out a huff as I grabbed my bag. Across the square, Lydia watched Maël disappear around the corner, her expression dripping with undisguised longing.

She leaned over to her friend and whispered something in her ear before heading my way, her lips curved into a predatory smile. I shoved my book back into my bag, preparing to avoid whatever was to come, but Lydia invaded my space before I could escape.

"You know," Lydia said, her voice dripping honey-sweet venom, "it's not proper to chase after another girl's man." Behind her, her friend tittered like a trained songbird.

My eyes narrowed. "You need to learn the definition of 'chase'" I spat, "because I certainly haven't been chasing anyone but the doe in the woods."

Lydia huffed and crossed her arms, her perfectly manicured nails digging into her arms. "Stay away from Maël, he's tired of you following him around like a lost puppy. He's just too nice to say anything about it."

A laugh burst from my throat, sharp and brittle as winter frost. Her attempt to scare me away was laughable in its desperation.

The irony wasn't lost on me—watching her catch Maël's attention had been torture enough, but now I had to endure her petty threats?

"If that's what Maël wants," I said, my voice as cold as midwinter frost despite the way my heart cracked, "then by all means, claim your prize."

I turned away before they could glimpse the weakness in my eyes and fled to the sanctuary of home.

CHAPTER 2

"Lor," my grandmother called from her garden as I approached our little cottage. A smile tugged at my lips as I veered slightly left onto the narrow dirt path, the gateway to her sanctuary.

I found her towards the center, her hands working deftly to pick tiny blue blooms from the bed she knelt before, her basket overflowing with freshly gathered herbs at her side. The late afternoon sun cast long shadows through the leaves above, dancing across her silver hair as butterflies and bees lazily drifted between the fragrant blooms surrounding her.

"Grandmother," I said, coming to a stop before her. She looked up, and I froze. Her face bore a resignation I'd only witnessed at funerals or when someone sought her aid for a grave illness. My heart clenched, a cold weight settling in my chest.

She waved me off. "I just needed ya to help an old bat up. Wrenched my ankle on that blasted rock," she gestured at a large stone near her basket, "and thought I'd finish picking these elder blooms while I waited for ya to return." She plucked a final bloom brushed her soil-stained hands on her apron, and reached towards me, her weathered hand extending toward mine.

I helped lift her up, bringing my shoulder under her arm to steady her. We took small steps towards the front door, her botanical treasures gripped in her free hand. Even with support, she winced with each step. Once I got her inside, I eased her into our kitchen, to a wooden chair at our little table.

"Get me a bowl and some water and jars so I can start on these, would ya dear?"

I nodded and started pulling the items she needed, setting them before her. She began sorting through her harvest, meticulously separating each plant, her practiced fingers sorting chamomile from elderflower with swift precision. The mingled scent of earth and herbs filled our small kitchen, a gentler echo of her garden's wild perfume.

"I need ya to go into town," she said suddenly. I halted as water splashed into the bowl before me, my hand frozen mid-pour. She'd never let me leave the vicinity of our little village, the surrounding woods marking the boundary of my permitted wanderings. *It's not safe, girl. Dangers lurk at every corner. I just want ya to be safe* - her constant refrain whenever I mentioned traveling. Truth be told, few ventured to the next town over. Most relied on our regular merchant for trade, but he hadn't been seen in over a fortnight. I stopped the water's flow, wiped the bowl's sides clean, and placed it on the table before her.

"You're allowing me to leave?" I whispered, hating how small my voice sounded. The countless nights I'd spent dreaming of far-off worlds and captivating adventures could fill volumes, each one ending with the bittersweet knowledge that my life would never reach such greatness. "What changed to make it safe now?" I asked, my fingers fidgeting with my shirt hem.

She sighed as she continued to sort through her herbs. "Sometimes fate has other plans. I couldn't get out of my garden on my own, much less travel over to Willowbrook. That blasted merchant hasn't been around for weeks. I need ya to fetch me some supplies from the apothecary there. Won't take more than a day to get there and back." She rummaged around in her apron until she found a crumpled piece of parchment. With shaking hands, she placed the list of items and a pouch of coins before me. "For the love of the old gods, be careful, girl. And take the lad with you—your wandering feet have gotten you lost in our own backyard."

I nodded, snatched my bag, and hurried out the door, grateful for the early success of my morning hunt and the abundant daylight ahead. My feet carried me through the village in search of Maël. The memory of Lydia's accusations about my "chasing" Maël surfaced unbidden. Her words had planted seeds of doubt that sprouted into thorny questions: Would he side with her? Was he simply too kind to push me away? Did our friendship mean as much to him as it did to me?

I spotted Maël with the blacksmith, the ends of his brown hair damp from training. He was bent over studying a blade when I approached them. The heat from the forge had left a sheen of sweat on his neck, the muscles in his arms taut as he examined the weapon's edge.

"Twice in one day, Lor, are you finally ready for our next sparring match?" He flashed a cocky smirk my way as he set the sword down.

I huffed. "Not unless you plan on a fair fight." The dirty cheat kicked dirt in my face and took me down at the knees last time. I hadn't sparred with him since, mostly on principle. "I need you to escort me to Willowbrook."

"Willowbrook? Eleni is letting you out of her sight?" His brow furrowed, his expression mirroring the disbelief churning in my own gut. Even if it was a short distance.

"We're going on her orders," I grabbed his arm and started pulling him to the main village gate. "Now come on, we've got to get going."

He pulled his arm free and crossed both in front of his chest. "And why should I risk life and limb for your grandmother's errands?"

I groaned in exasperation. "Come on, Maël. Everyone else has seen beyond these trees except me. Even you've been to Willowbrook before."

I didn't wait for his response. Permission or not, I was going.

His rich laugh warmed the air as he fell into step beside me. "If you think Willowbrook counts as an adventure, you really need to get out more." His teasing only made my heart flutter traitorously in my chest, a reaction I desperately tried to ignore. His long legs had him caught up to me within a few paces. He took a hand and ruffled the top of my hair, "But who am I to refuse the great Eleni's summons?"

"Demand is more like it..."

"Tomato, potato," he waved me off with a hand, "Just try to keep up and stay close. I'm not wasting my afternoon hunting for you in the woods."

"If I get lost, and that's a big if," I stuck my tongue out at him.

He nudges me with his shoulder as we enter the woods, "With you Lor, it's always when. When you get lost, I'll lead you home." The ancient trees loomed before us, their gnarled branches reaching to the sky like grasping fingers. Dappled sunlight filtered through the dense canopy, casting an ethereal glow on the moss-covered forest floor.

EXCITEMENT THRUMMED THROUGH MY VEINS, threatening to burst free like wildfire through dry brush.

Willowbrook made our village look like a child's toy, unfurling before us like a living tapestry. Stone and timber buildings marched in neat rows along the paved streets. Gardens overflowed with late summer blooms, while rainbow-hued laundry danced on lines above. Children darted between market-goers like mischievous sprites, their laughter carried on the breeze.

The market square opened before us like a jewel box.

Navy and violet banners adorned each shop front, embroidered with silvery crescent moons and twinkling stars. The square pulsed with an energy so different from our sleepy village center.

Merchants called their wares while townspeople haggled and gossiped at every stall.

Spices and fresh-baked bread perfumed the air, making my stomach growl as we wandered the market.

Wooden stalls crowded the cobblestone path, pressed against a line of weathered stone shops.

I couldn't help but smile as I stopped to look at the trinkets. Maël's attention caught on a weapons vendor displaying an array of deadly-looking blades, including some I'd never seen before - perfectly circular and gleaming.

"An Esmeranian specialty," the old man said with pride, "they're meant to be thrown, faster than an arrow and as sharp as any blade."

I watched Maël turn the weapon in his hands, admiring how his fingers traced the deadly edge. He bargained like a seasoned merchant, all easy charm and calculated pauses.

We'd stepped into a world that felt alien, yet oddly alluring. It wasn't just Willowbrook; it was the way people interacted with each other. Something inside me ached for this to be our reality.

In my mind's eye, I saw us here—sharing drinks at the tavern, breaking warm bread from the bakery, our lives woven into the fabric of this place. Under the sprawling willow tree in the market's heart, we could share meals and spin stories about the travelers passing through, imagining their destinations and the tales they carried.

My chest tightened with wanting—for him, for this life, for all the possibilities that seemed forever just beyond my grasp.

Maël caught me staring at him and gave me a lopsided grin. "What were you thinking about?" he asked, his voice low and husky.

I blushed fiercely, feeling my cheeks burn under his gaze. "Nothing," I muttered, looking away.

He laughed, the sound warm and rich, as he caught my hand and drew me near. His scent of leather and pine washed over me, the late summer breeze carrying whispers of metal and sun warmed skin. The heat of his palm against mine made my breath catch, a dangerous dance of friendship and something more.

"Come on," he said, "let's head over to the apothecary for your grandmother."

His calloused fingers threaded through mine, each point of contact sending sparks racing along my skin as we made our way to the apothecary. My heart fluttered beneath my ribs, every nerve ending alive to the rough warmth of his palm against mine, the gentle sweep of his thumb across my knuckles making my breath catch in my throat.

He saw me to the shop's entrance, making some excuse about another errand. I tried not to wonder if he was off to examine more weapons or if the tavern's warmth—and its patrons—had caught his eye.

I forced the jealous thoughts away, clinging instead to the lingering warmth of his touch and the impossible dreams it sparked.

CHAPTER 3

I stepped inside the musty apothecary. The scent of herbs and flowers overwhelmed my senses. Dried lavender and sage hung from the rafters in neat bundles, while the sharp bite of crushed mint and the earthy musk of mushrooms danced in the air. As I entered, a woman with sharp features and piercing blue eyes looked up from her work. She watched me expectantly as I rummaged through my bag.

"What can I do for you?" she asked, her tone not welcoming.

"I need these for my grandmother," I passed her the list of ingredients. "She was sure you'd carry them."

She took the parchment, reviewing my grandmother's careful script. "Your grandmother wouldn't happen to be Eleni, would she?"

The woman's sharp stare left me speechless. Her gaze pierced through me like a winter frost, sharp and unforgiving. It seemed like my grandmother had crossed her in the past. Knowing her, she probably did. I crossed my arms, fighting the urge to defend her reputation right there. My grandmother was equal parts maddening and merciful.

I nodded, unable to speak a word. The owner rolled her eyes as she pushed past a curtain at her back, muttering something about young people and no manners as she disappeared.

While waiting for her to gather the items, my eyes wandered around the shop. Dusty shelves overflowed with glass jars containing liquids of various colors, some containing ingredients like eye of newt or toadstools. The air hung thick with notes of smoke and rosemary. My attention caught on a shelf full of worn leather books, their gilded letters along the spines worn with age and in a language I couldn't quite make out. A thump at the counter drew my attention back, and I found the owner had returned with a thick parcel.

"It'll be five silvers for everything, tell your grandmother I gave you her usual discount."

I smiled and retrieved the coins from the pouch in my bag, handing them to her. "Thank you."

Just as I was about to leave with the goods in hand, the owner spoke again. "Your grandmother has always been an enigma to me," she said thoughtfully. "She's never shared much about herself, but she always comes with a tale of her granddaughter. It makes me miss my own greatly."

I gave her a small smile as I grabbed my wares and headed towards the door, feeling a pang of sadness at the thought of there ever being a day when I wouldn't wake up to my grandmother busying herself in our home. She was the only family I had in this life.

The moment I stepped back into the sunlight, my breath caught in my throat. Maël stood before a jeweler's shop next door, a glinting ring held delicately between his fingers. My fingers trembled against the parcel in my hands, my chest constricting as though wrapped in thorny vines. The world seemed to narrow, darkening at the edges as I stared at that cursed ring, my mouth going dry as dust.

My heart sank as realization dawned on me. Was he planning to propose? And to whom? A shiver ran down my spine, thinking about the moment with Lydia I witnessed earlier. The thought of him proposing made me feel sick inside. Just moments ago, I had been imagining a childish future with him while he had plans with another. It was never going to be me and Maël. My chest hollowed, each breath a battle against the void threatening to consume me. The ring's gleam mocked every stolen glance, every lingering touch, every moment I'd foolishly treasured between us. I was nothing but a shadow in his light, destined to watch from the darkness as he chose another.

Desperate to escape the crushing weight of reality, I slipped into the nearest alley, my feet carrying me around the square until I found myself at the tavern's door.

I needed to numb myself to the bitter truth that had shattered my heart.

I claimed a dark corner table, where the flickering candlelight couldn't reach.

The barmaid barely glanced at my face before returning with a pitcher of dark wine.

I let the wine burn away my thoughts, while the tavern's cheerful chaos mocked my misery.

Perhaps at the bottom of this pitcher, I'd find the strength to forget his smile.

THE WINE FLOWED like liquid courage through my veins. The tavern had erupted into a cacophony of laughter and song since my arrival. Seeking solace in another tankard of wine, as merrymakers celebrated life's fleeting joys. Would Grandmother's disapproving frown greet me when she learned I'd spent my first taste of freedom drowning in wine and self-pity?

Perhaps. But did the weight of her judgment compare to the crushing pain in my chest? Honestly, not in that moment.

Maël would eventually track me down, drag me back. We'd go back to our separate lives, as destiny seemed to demand.

Maël...Maël and his ring. Soon to be Maël and his fiancée. I gulped down more wine, pressing my palms against my eyes until stars burst behind my lids. I'd have to paste on a smile while our entire village celebrated his happiness with another. Oh gods, I'd have to stand there, frozen in my personal hell, watching him pledge himself to another.

The wine scorched a path down my throat, a blessed burn to rival the one in my chest. My fingers trembled against the tankard's surface, my usually steady hands betraying me now. The tavern's cheerful atmosphere felt like a cruel joke, mocking my misery with each peal of mirth that rang out, each clink of tankards an echo of my shattering heart.

I could see him there, his tall frame commanding attention against the backdrop of a perfect day. Maël would be effortlessly handsome, as always, his brown eyes dancing with joy as he beheld his radiant bride. A bride who wouldn't be me. I'd be there in the crowd, suffocating on unsaid words.

While everyone else celebrated the happiest day of my best friend's life, I'd be drowning in my own misery.

My violet eyes would be rimmed with red, each exchanged vow another crack in my already splintering heart. Gods, I was pathetic.

I'd ruined everything. Somewhere between the quiet moments and shared laughs, I'd started dreaming of more than friendship. My beloved books had betrayed me, filling my head with tales of friends becoming lovers until my foolish heart believed I could have that too.

That Maël and I could be more than what we were. Nothing but a fairytale I'd spun in the quiet moments between duties and hunts.

The bitter taste of wine only emphasized my foolishness.

How could Maël, with his warm heart and easy smile, ever want someone as sharp-edged as me? Like morning mist dissolving in sunlight, some dreams were never meant to last.

Having nearly finished my current glass, I contemplated ordering another drink when a pair of strangers materialized at my table like shadows. One loomed like a scarecrow while his companion was built like a boulder. They wore clothes dulled by road dust and time, but there was something predatory about them I couldn't pin down in my drunken haze.

"Evening, miss," the taller one said, flashing a smile that didn't reach his eyes. "Care if we join you?"

I waved a hand lazily, gesturing to the empty chairs. "Suit yourselves."

They sat, and the shorter one leaned in, his breath carrying the stale scent of ale.

"We're merchants, you see. Looking for a small village nearby to peddle our wares. You wouldn't happen to know of any, would you?"

My wine-addled mind perked up at the word 'wares.' "Merchants? What kind of goods do you sell?" The flickering tavern light cast strange shadows across their faces, highlighting a thin scar on the tall one's jaw. The shorter one's thick fingers drummed an uneven rhythm on the wooden table. Even through my drunken state, something about them set off warning bells in my head, but the wine made it all too easy to dismiss.

"Oh, a bit of everything," the tall one said, his words as slippery as oil. "Blades, books, clothing—treasures for every taste."

The promise of new books—fresh escapes from this reality where Maël belonged to someone else—made my shattered heart leap.

"What sort of books?" I asked, leaning forward despite the way the room tilted.

The shorter one's grin widened, revealing teeth too sharp for comfort. "Oh, everything a young lady might desire. Romance, adventure, mystery—stories to make your wildest dreams come true."

The wine pushed words past my lips before wisdom could catch them. "There's a village not far from here. Half a day's walk southwest. It's home."

"Is that so?" The tall one's eyes gleamed like a wolf's in moonlight. "And this village has a name?"

"Briarwood. It's small," I added, the wine making me generous with secrets, "but we welcome visitors. Especially those bearing quality goods."

The men shared a look that should have terrified me, had I been sober enough to read it. "Well, aren't you helpful?" the tall one purred. "We'll be sure to visit your little village soon with our... special merchandise."

As they melted into the tavern's shadows, I called after them, "Remember the books!" My words chased their retreating forms like a child's wish thrown into a well.

They chuckled, a sound that should've sent chills down my spine. "Oh, we won't forget. Not at all."

The men slipped away, their laughter trailing behind them like smoke. I felt my cheeks warm from the wine and the conversation. Unease curled in my gut. Briarwood had always welcomed strangers with open arms, yet something about those two felt off. I shook my head, trying to clear the drunken fog as I took another swig from my tankard.

Suddenly, the tavern door swung open, and of course it was Maël. He stood tall against the warm glow of lantern light, scanning the room with an ease that made me smile despite myself. My heart skipped a beat when our eyes locked.

He made his way over, brow furrowed with concern. "Lor," he said softly, slipping into that familiar tone that sent a shiver down my spine. "You alright?"

"Just fine," I replied too quickly, trying to hide how far gone I really was.

He leaned closer, his brown eyes narrowing as he assessed me. "You've had enough for one night." His voice held that gentle authority I couldn't resist.

"Maybe I just wanted to celebrate," I shot back, bitterness creeping into my words.

"Celebrate what? Your ability to drink like a fish?" A hint of teasing danced in his tone, but his words fell flat against the weight crushing my chest.

I tried to look away but found myself trapped by those warm brown eyes.

The ring he'd purchased haunted my thoughts, a dark storm threatening to drown me.

Maël's lips twisted into a frown as he held me with a gentle grip when I swayed.

"We should get you home."

I stumbled as we stepped outside, the cool night air hitting me like a splash of cold water. My vision blurred as he steadied me against his solid frame.

"Alora." His voice softened with concern. "What's going on? You can tell me anything."

I opened my mouth but managed only a whisper, the words clinging to the edges of wine and despair.

"I just had a little too much, apparently I can't hold my liquor."

He rolled his eyes, wrapping an arm around my waist as we started home. The rhythm of our steps lulled me, my head growing heavy against his shoulder.

"Next time, you're carrying my drunk ass home," he muttered, before sweeping me into his arms, one hand beneath my knees, the other supporting my back.

I nestled against his shoulder, breathing in his familiar scent—pine needles and home.

"I just wish..." My voice faded to barely a whisper, "...you'd choose me."

I swore his grip tightened around me before darkness claimed me.

CHAPTER 4

The morning sun peeked through the trees, bathing the camp in a soft glow that felt too bright against my throbbing head. I cracked my eyes open, squinting at the light. Pain pulsed through my temples like a hammer striking an anvil. Shadows danced at the edges of my vision, each pulse of pain bringing with it memories of last night's mistakes, sharp and bitter as poison.

"Good morning." Maël's voice cut through the fog, lighthearted yet tinged with something deeper. He leaned against a nearby tree, arms crossed and an amused smirk on his face. My traitorous heart skipped a beat at the sight of him, all lean muscle and casual grace, and I hated how even in my miserable state, I couldn't help but notice the way his shirt clung to his shoulders.

I groaned and buried my face in my hands. "Ugh, your voice is like nails digging into my skull." My tongue felt like lead, heavy and useless in my parched mouth.

He chuckled softly, moving closer. "You really overdid it last night. I thought I'd have to carry you home if we hadn't stopped for the night." The thought of his arms around me sent an unwelcome shiver down my spine, and I cursed my weakness for him.

"Thanks for the reminder," I muttered, forcing myself to sit up. The world tilted like a ship in a storm, and I swallowed hard against the bile rising in my throat.

"You sure you're alright?" He crouched beside me, concern etched in his features. "Maybe you should drink some water or—"

"I'm fine!" I snarled, the words clawing their way out of my throat like angry beasts. My voice was raw and jagged as broken glass, each syllable dripping with the venom of my hangover and wounded pride.

Maël jerked back at my outburst, his eyebrows climbing toward his hairline.

"Maybe if you stopped hovering like a worried mother hen," I shot back, my words sharp as daggers.

His expression hardened as he straightened up, crossing his arms across his chest.

"You're awfully venomous for someone I had to take care of all night. You could just say a simple thank you."

"I didn't ask you to take care of me," I spat, the words tasting like ash in my mouth.

"You didn't have to." His voice was quiet, all traces of humor now gone.

"Well, next time, leave me in a ditch somewhere!" The words burst from my lips like poison arrows, my vulnerability bleeding through despite my best efforts.

The moment the words escaped, regret wrapped around my heart like a poisoned barb. His concern, his care... gods, I yearned for it like a dying breath. The memory of what led me to drink so much tore through my thoughts like shattered glass. It'd be better to push him away than witness him fall for another. Better, but it felt like plunging a blade between my own ribs.

"Getting drunk won't fix what's eating at you, Lor. I just wish you'd talk to me."

"Save your wisdom for someone who wants it."

I stormed off toward our path home, rage and regret warring with each step, neither winning nor yielding ground.

Our journey was deadly quiet from then on. The silence stretched uncomfortably between us, heavy as a gravestone. By the time we reached Briarwood, fatigue gnawed at my bones with each twist of the path.

My grandmother's cottage came into view, a haven of despite the storm between us.

As I stepped inside with Maël following close behind, the familiar perfume of dried herbs wrapped around me, sweet as mercy. My grandmother stood by the hearth, hands on her hips as she eyed me suspiciously.

"Where have you been?" she asked sharply, noticing my disheveled appearance.

"Just gathering your herbs." I fumbled for the small pouch slung across my shoulder and handed it over.

"You reek like a tavern after a brawl."

Shame turned my silver tongue to lead, my usual wit deserting me like shadows at dawn. Pride and guilt tangled in my throat, strangling any defense I might have made.

"Go sleep it off, you're no use to anyone all hungover," she commanded gently yet firmly, waving me away before turning her attention back to her herbs.

With a growl that was more wounded animal than human, I dragged myself upstairs, leaving Maël at the threshold, his concern a weight heavier than my hangover.

Each step brought fresh waves of nausea, accompanied by echoes of disappointment—my grandmother's words, Maël's worried eyes.

Something fragile in my chest begged me to turn back, to let down my walls for him. But the fortress I'd built around my heart stood firm.

It was easier to be alone than to risk the pain of rejection, even if that loneliness cut deeper than any blade.

I WOKE up to the sun creeping through the cracks in my window, the harsh light piercing my throbbing skull. The memory of my grandmother's voice echoed in my mind, her stern tone from earlier lingering like an unwanted guest.

With a grunt, I rolled out of bed and stumbled toward the kitchen. My grandmother stood at the hearth, stirring a pot. I gravitated toward its savory aroma like a moth to a flame.

"You're alive," she said without looking up. "How's your head?"

I rubbed my temples, letting out a noncommittal grunt. "It's fine."

She paused, finally glancing at me with that look only grandmothers seem to possess. "You're not the best liar, ya know. Why don't you do something to fix that?"

I leaned against the doorframe, crossing my arms defensively. "What do you suggest? A walk? A little tea?"

"Training with the guards," she said simply, stirring the pot with renewed vigor.

"Training?" I frowned. The thought of swinging swords while feeling like I'd been run over by a cart didn't sound appealing.

"Did I stutter? Yes, training," she snapped back, waving her hand dismissively. "It'll help you work out whatever's eating at you."

I let out a weary breath but knew better than to argue. After a quick change into my fighting leathers, I trudged outside, where the training ring loomed ahead on the village outskirts.

The sun beat down mercilessly overhead as I entered the training ring, forcing me to shield my eyes. Steel rang against steel, punctuated by shouts of encouragement that made my head pound.

I scanned the familiar faces of villagers as they trained, their movements watched by stern-eyed instructors.

Then I saw him. Maël. His skin glistened with sweat as he sparred with a village guard, each movement showcasing his skill.

His movements were swift and sure, each strike purposeful. A knot formed in my stomach as I watched him effortlessly disarm his opponent, awakening emotions I refused to name.

Frustration churned beneath my skin like a storm waiting to break as I strode over to the pile of discarded weapons. I chose a shorter blade from the pile, knowing my speed would have to compensate for what I lacked in brute strength.

"Alora!" a guard called out as he wiped his brow with his forearm. "Over here!"

I clenched my jaw, forcing a sharp nod as I stalked towards the guards. The guards encircled me, their eyes alight with the promise of violence.

The guards quickly paired off, and adrenaline surged through my veins as I sparred with a young villager called Finn.

Steel met steel as Finn pressed forward with surprising grace, forcing me back until raw instinct claimed control.

My body moved on its own, unleashing a storm of strikes that caught even me off guard, muscle memory taking command where conscious thought failed.

Though I lacked their years of training, I held my ground with a fierce determination that made up for my inexperience.

The crowd's cheers fueled our deadly dance as we circled each other, our blades singing their lethal song. Like wraiths locked in an eternal waltz, we moved through the afternoon light, our blades weaving patterns of death and glory.

Yet every glance towards Maël sent fury ripping through my chest, tearing open scars I'd foolishly thought I could ignore.

There he stood, radiating joy in his element, untouched by the shadows of our recent misadventure. Of course he'd be fine—winning his matches, probably planning his next encounter with Lydia or whoever else had caught his wandering heart.

"Better stay focused," Finn teased, dancing away from my blade.

Teeth clenched, I surged forward, but Finn moved like smoke through my fingers, and my balance betrayed me. His leg swept beneath mine, and the world tilted. My back slammed against the dirt with a sound that spoke of wounded pride more than pain.

Laughter exploded around the ring, shame burning through my veins like liquid fire.

Maël's laugh cut through the chaos, twisting deeper into my already bleeding pride. My pulse thundered with more than just humiliation—rage coiled in my chest, aimed at him and his casual cruelty in finding joy in my failure.

Fury unfurled inside me like a serpent tasting the air. "Alright!" I called out, my voice cutting through their laughter like a blade. "Who's next?"

The laughter died abruptly as a massive figure strode into the ring. Galen, our head trainer, towered over me, his scarred face etched with stern determination.

"I'll take you on, Alora," he said, his voice gruff. "Let's see what you've got."

My heart raced with equal parts dread and excitement. Galen was legendary, his brutal training methods and unmatched prowess the stuff of village whispers. He fought with the ferocity of a cornered beast, relentless and merciless. Yet, in that moment, I'd have faced a hundred Galens rather than endure another second of Maël's mocking laughter.

A feral growl rumbled in my chest as I hefted my practice sword, steeling myself to face the beast before me.

Galen circled me slowly, his eyes never leaving mine. I matched his movements, trying to anticipate his first strike. The forest had been my hunting ground for years, but under Galen's predatory gaze, I suddenly understood what it meant to be prey.

"Widen your stance," he barked suddenly. "You're off balance."

I adjusted quickly, feeling the difference immediately. Galen nodded approvingly before lunging forward with lightning speed. I barely managed to parry his blow, the force of it sending shockwaves up my arm.

"Good reflexes. There's hope for you yet," he grunted. "Now, attack."

I launched forward, feinting left before my blade whistled toward his right. Galen deflected the blow with ease, but beneath his mask of boredom, I caught a flicker of approval in his eyes.

With each clash of steel, my anger at Maël began to unravel. My mind cleared despite the surge of emotions—the sting of his words, the pain of his impending marriage, the knowledge that I was losing him forever. Beneath my fury lurked guilt; he'd only tried to help my drunken self, and I'd repaid his kindness with venom.

Galen's approval shouldn't have mattered. What I truly wanted was to see him taste defeat as I had. The thought brought a bitter satisfaction I wasn't proud of, but couldn't quite shake.

Before I knew it, the world tilted, and suddenly I was on my back, the impact driving the air from my lungs.

"Better," he said. "But you're giving away your moves to your opponent. Keep your shoulders relaxed." Galen's criticism landed differently than Maël's ever had—like a sword striking true rather than an arrow finding a weak spot. My jaw unclenched slightly as his gruff voice washed over me, carrying none of the playful mockery that always colored Maël's "helpful suggestions." Instead, there was only the steady weight of experience behind his words, and somehow that made them easier to bear.

We continued to trade blows as Galen barked out instructions.

My muscles screamed in protest, sweat stinging my eyes, but I refused to yield. With each exchange, I felt myself improving, my movements becoming more fluid and purposeful.

My blade traced tighter arcs now, each strike finding its mark with newfound precision. Where before I'd swung wildly, now my attacks flowed like water—one movement bleeding seamlessly into the next. The practice sword became an extension of my arm rather than just a clumsy weight, and I caught myself anticipating Galen's counters before he made them. When he struck high, I was already moving low, and when he feinted left, I read the tension in his shoulders that betrayed his true intent.

"Watch your footwork!" Galen called out as he pressed forward with a series of quick jabs. I danced backward, narrowly avoiding his blade. The packed earth shifted beneath my feet, each step accompanied by the sharp ring of steel slicing through air.

As my arms trembled with exhaustion, Galen lowered his sword. "Enough for today," he declared.

I blinked, becoming aware of the gathered crowd, their faces painted with surprise and admiration. I caught a glimpse of Maël's impressed expression before forcing my gaze away.

"Alright, enough chatter!" Galen's voice thundered across the training grounds. "War comes without warning, and from what I've seen today, most of you would fall in your first real battle. To your watch shifts—dismissed!"

The guards scattered like startled birds, their earlier bravado dissolving into hushed murmurs as they returned to their posts.

Maël remained rooted in place, his gaze shrouded with a mysterious heaviness.

"Move it," Galen barked, his scarred face darkening. Maël finally sauntered away, leaving me alone in the ring with our battle-hardened trainer.

Galen stepped closer, his shadow looming over me like a

mountain. He extended a calloused hand toward me. "On your feet, Lor."

I grasped his hand, wincing as he yanked me to my feet. My legs trembled beneath me as I brushed the sweat from my eyes.

"Focus," he said sharply. "Don't let your emotions guide you in a fight. It clouds your judgment and could get you killed."

I bit back a retort and nodded, though my pride still stung. It wasn't as if I'd ever be in a life or death battle. I wasn't a guard, after all. The worst I'd face was a territorial bear, and I doubted it cared about proper sword technique.

"Years ago," he began, his gaze unwavered, "I was just a soldier in the war. Our platoon often traveled for days at a time. I never understood what it meant to be at my limits until then." His voice dropped an octave as he continued, "One day, we were ambushed. Surrounded on all sides, we had no choice but to stand our ground. I lost friends that day, brothers."

I shifted uncomfortably under his intense stare, feeling the weight of his words.

"But I learned something," he went on, folding his arms across his chest as if to shield himself from the memories. "When it comes down to it, your heart can be your greatest weapon or your worst enemy. I was consumed by an argument I'd had with the captain earlier about pushing on at our grueling pace. He died beside me while I was too angry to even glance his way. I should have been checking if he needed help, my anger and pride got in the way of that. You have to take control or else you won't see what's right in front of you." His words hit too close to home, stirring thoughts of Maël that I desperately wanted to ignore.

"Why are you here then? The war still rages beyond our borders." The question slipped out before I could hold it back.

He met my gaze directly. "We fought until we fell. I was the only survivor, they likely thought I was dead when all they did was knock me out. I stumbled into the woods, searching for the men who slaughtered my brothers. When I found this village after everything ended... well, I knew these people would need protection one day. They took me in, your grandmother healed me, and I vowed to train them in case the war came to their doorsteps." He shrugged slightly as if dismissing the significance of his choice, but I felt its weight settle between us. "And it will. This war has raged for too long to spare even havens like Briarwood."

The training yard slowly filled with noise again as he walked away, leaving me alone with the ghosts of his past and the shadows of my own thoughts.

CHAPTER 5

I roamed through the forest hunting, the quiet of the woods calming the storm in my mind. The setting sun painted long shadows across the path as I neared my grandmother's cottage. The day was fading into twilight, darkness creeping between the trees.

The familiar scent of earth and blooming wildflowers filled the air, but tonight, unease lingered beneath the surface. The conversation with Galen twisted through my thoughts. The memory of my match with Finn burned fresh, especially with Maël's appearance and his taunting words still ringing in my ears.

As I stepped onto the worn path leading to the door, something caught my eye. There, on the doorstep, lay a book. The golden title inlaid in the worn green cover shone under the fading sunlight. My pulse jumped at the sight. There was no doubt in my mind that Maël had left it. An offering of peace.

I knelt down, fingers brushing over the spine. The worn leather beneath my fingers felt like an echo of his touch. A reminder of all those times we'd sprawled on the grass together. I'd share my stories with him and he his dreams of being a valiant knight. I glanced around, half-expecting him to appear from behind a tree, his usual playful grin plastered on his face. But nothing stirred but the gentle rustle of leaves.

Exhaling a breath that carried both relief and frustration, I tucked the book under my arm and slipped inside the cottage. The dim glow of candlelight flickered against the walls, casting playful shadows that danced as if they shared my thoughts.

Once settled in bed, I opened the book, revealing familiar scrawls across yellowing pages. Illustrations of trees and mountains, even wolves and snakes curled around paragraphs and quotes. It told of a lost girl who encountered both danger and salvation in the woods - a deceitful snake and a protective wolf. While I normally wouldn't condone defacing any book, Maël's sketches seemed to fit, as if this book would never have existed without them.

Each sketch brought a bittersweet ache. My heart and mind clashed over whether this gift was merely a peace offering or something deeper.

I curled onto my side, hugging the book to my chest like armor against my turbulent thoughts. Moonlight streamed through the window, catching dust motes that twirled like my scattered emotions. The pages held echoes of us—shared laughter on long sunny days and secrets whispered through winter nights. Like a rope in stormy seas, I clung to these memories, even as I feared the weight of them might pull me under.

Sleep claimed me as one final question lingered: what message lay hidden between these marked pages?

MORNING LIGHT SEEPED through the cracks in the shutters, but something felt off. I blinked awake, my body heavy with an peculiar sense of foreboding. The usual sound of my grandmother bustling about in the kitchen wasn't there. I pushed the covers aside and swung my legs over the side of the bed, my heart pounding in my chest.

"Grandmother?" My voice pierced the stillness. I hastily pulled on my leathers. I padded down the small hallway to the kitchen, but it remained silent. The usual morning symphony of clattering pots and sweet aromas was absent.

Vacant. Loneliness pressed against my chest like a physical weight.

I stepped outside into the cool morning air, hoping maybe she had ventured into town or taken to her garden early for herbs to ease her aching joints. But as I walked toward our bountiful garden, dread twisted inside me like dark clouds rolling over an otherwise clear sky.

I turned back toward town, an impulse rising within me to find Maël. I owed him one hell of an apology, even if it meant enduring his teasing again. The thought brought a small smile to my lips amid churning worry.

As I moved through the village, people bustled about their morning routines but their joy felt distant from where I stood. With each step toward Maël's usual haunt near the square, determination coursed within me.

I spotted him leaning against the weathered fence of the training ring, laughing with a group of friends while his brown hair caught glimmers of sunlight. The sight of him made my heart flutter— comfort and chaos wrapped in one effortlessly charming package.

"Maël!" My voice cut through their chatter like a knife through fog, urgent and clear amidst all that noise surrounding us.

His friends quieted as they all turned to look at me. Among them was Finn, who sneered at the sight of me.

"Well, if it isn't the vicious little hunter," Maël teased, a mischievous grin spreading across his face, "Finn just got his ass handed to him by

Thomas, I'm sure he could use another easy win." The boys snickered around them and Finn's face flushed crimson with anger. I took the comment at face value, not letting it turn my emotions into another rage. I smiled up at Maël as if he had said the most wonderful thing to me.

I knew gushing about the book or apologizing right here in front of everyone wouldn't bode well for either of us. The boys were like vultures if you showed any signs of weakness. Poor Thomas let it slip he was sweet on a girl and they had tormented him for months.

"How about you and me, Maël?" I challenged, my violet eyes locking onto his brown ones. A spark of anticipation flickered in their depths. The others fell silent, sensing the shift in atmosphere as Maël's grin faltered for a heartbeat.

Maël's eyes widened, his confident grin faltering for a moment. "You want to spar with me?" His tone carried equal measures of surprise and intrigue, a challenge sparking in his eyes.

I nodded, my violet eyes locked on his. "Afraid you can't keep up?"

The men around us let out a chorus of "ooohs," egging him on. Maël's shock melted into a wicked smirk. "Alright, Lor. Let's see what you've got."

We stepped into the ring, stalking each other in measured steps. My heart raced, but not from fear. This was familiar territory. This dance with him was all too familiar.

Maël struck first, a quick jab that I evaded with practiced ease. I countered with a sweep of my leg, nearly catching him off guard. He stumbled but regained his footing, chuckling. "Getting better, little hunter."

A thin sheen of sweat formed on my skin as I blocked a particularly fierce punch. Maël was strong, but I was quick. His raw strength met my speed, and I landed two strikes for each of his.

The world narrowed to just us, the men's roars becoming distant echoes. I saw an opening and went for it, launching a kick toward his center. But Maël was ready. He caught my ankle, turning my own force against me.

I hit the ground hard with a heavy thud, the breath knocked from my lungs, my ribs screaming in protest as dirt and gravel bit into my back.

Before I could recover, Maël had me pinned, his weight pressing me into the dirt.

"Yield?" he breathed, his face inches from mine.

I struggled for a moment, but his grip was unbreakable. "I yield," I panted.

Maël pulled away and reached down to help me. As he pulled me up, I expected to see triumph in his eyes. Instead, there was only warmth and genuine concern.

"Good match," he said gently.

I nodded, trying to steady my breathing. "Thank you. And... thank you for the book. It was thoughtful." My heart fluttered traitorously in my chest, warmth spreading through me despite the ache of my bruised pride.

Maël's expression grew tender. "You're welcome, Lor."

I swallowed hard, pushing down my pride. "I'm sorry about our argument. I shouldn't have snapped at you like that."

He traced his jaw thoughtfully, watching as the rowdy boys sauntered away now that the match had concluded. "It's alright, I just wish you'd talk to me when something is wrong."

I lowered my gaze to my feet, the truth lodged in my throat like a thorn. "It was just too much wine. You know I don't have much experience." I lied, it was the only way I could think to patch things up without revealing I drunk myself into oblivion over him.

"Well, seems your tolerance for wine rivals your sense of direction." He nudged my shoulder, his laugh deep and warm. "Trenton ditched patrol duty tonight. Care to join me instead?"

My heart leapt at the prospect, but I forced my expression to remain neutral. "And what's in it for me? I'm not keen on being your backup while you catch some shut-eye."

"Come on, Lor," he said, eyes sparkling with mischief. "It's your birthday, and I happen to know we'll be passing a merchant camp. Who knows? They might have a tragic romance to add to your collection."

"Fine," I conceded, trying to ignore the flutter in my chest.

His face lit up with my acceptance, a grin spreading across his features. "Perfect. I'll come by your place after supper."

As he turned to leave, I said, "I can just meet you at the front gate…"

He turned back, his eyebrows raised in mock horror. "And risk you getting lost? Not a chance. I'd rather face a pack of dire wolves than your grandmother's wrath. She'd break every bone in my body and make sure they all healed wrong." With a final grin and a casual wave, he sauntered off, no doubt to catch some rest before our night patrol.

I watched him go, my chest tightening with a familiar ache. Tears threatened to blur my vision, and I blinked them back angrily, hating myself for being so weak. This was Maël, my best friend, nothing more. But as I turned to leave, I couldn't shake the feeling that I was walking away from something far greater than just a patrol partner.

CHAPTER 6

When I returned home, Grandmother already had a stew simmering over the hearth. "You're finally back!" she called. "I was hoping I wouldn't have to send Maël to fetch ya."

I joined her by the hearth, adding the fresh meat she'd been waiting for. "He found me anyway, Grandmother. I swear, you terrify that man."

Her laugh tinkled like silver bells in the wind. "As it should be." I smiled, setting my gear aside.

Our cottage was modest but warm—a main room for living and cooking, two snug bedrooms, and a washroom. But the true magic lay in Grandmother's gardens just beyond our door, the most expansive and beautiful in the village, her pride and joy.

I sighed as I sat down, "Speaking of Maël, he needs a partner for tonight, so I'll be out with him until sunrise. I hope that's okay."

Grandmother paused as she considered my words. "Whatever ya need to do, Love, just try not to beat him up too badly. I'd rather spend the day with ya than mending his bruises."

I laughed at her mischievous expression. For all her strict rules—

stay near the village, don't venture too deep into the woods—when it came to my passion for hunting and combat, she was fiercely supportive.

She passed me a bowl of stew and settled in with her own. We ate in comfortable silence, though I caught her lost in thought more than once. After finishing, I gathered our bowls and began tidying up, debating whether I could steal a quick nap before Maël's arrival.

"Alora," my grandmother caught my attention. I peered over at her to see her fidgeting near the window, "Before you go, I'd like to give ya your gift a little early."

"Grandmother, you don't have to do that, I'll be back once the sun is risen and we will have all day for that."

She slowly nodded her head, "That may be, but as ya know, your powers will be manifesting soon, and I'd rather give you this now just in case." She held out a small bundle wrapped in a dark cloth.

I didn't process what she said as I unwrapped the cloth to find a dagger dark as night yet sparkling in the light, almost as if it had starlight embedded within it. "Where did this come from?" I gasped. I've never seen anything like it. It was so different, yet felt so familiar.

"It's been passed down from generation to generation," she began, "Keep it on ya in case you ever need it. Ya may find yourself vulnerable, and this could save your life one day." She flashed me a proud smile, "Or you'll use it on your hunts, just don't lose it."

I looked down at the blade again and back at the woman before me, "Thank you, I may get lost, but I will never let this out of my sight." I placed the blade in its sheath and strapped it to my thigh, "There, safe and sound."

She chuckled, shaking her head, a loving gesture that shows their close bond, knowing I would get lost a thousand times in our very own village and still manage to keep the knife safe.

Grandmother's eyes softened as she gazed at me, her weathered hands tenderly clasped mine. "Alora, my dear, the world beyond our village... it can be a cruel place. People aren't always kind, and life isn't always fair."

A frown creased my brow as memories of Maël at the jewelry shop surfaced. "I'm not some sheltered child."

"I know you're not, but knowing and experiencing it are two very different things." She paused, her violet eyes, mirrors of my own, searching my face. "You're strong, Alora. Stronger than you know. But even the strongest trees bend in the fiercest storms."

I swallowed hard, feeling the weight of her words. "What aren't you telling me?"

"I'm saying no matter what happens, you must keep your head up. Keep moving forward. The world may try to break you, but you, my dear, are unbreakable." Her voice grew fierce with conviction.

The intensity in her gaze made me straighten my spine. "I hear you, Grandmother."

I felt my throat tighten at the tender gesture. She nodded, seemingly satisfied. "Good. Remember, your strength isn't just in your blade or your fists. It's here," she tapped my chest, right above my heart, "and here," she touched my forehead gently. My breath caught at the gentle touch, and I fought the urge to wrap her in a fierce hug.

"I promise, Grandmother. I won't forget."

She smiled then, the lines around her eyes crinkling. "Now go wash up before that boy gets here. You're looking—and smelling— like you've been wrestling Ole Jenny's pigs."

I made my way to the little bathroom, truth be told, she probably wasn't wrong. The day's hunt had left its mark. The bath water was cool but bearable—no time to heat it properly. I slipped in and scrubbed away the day's grime. The water darkened as I worked the soap through my hair. Once clean, I dried myself and looked in the weathered mirror, my own deep violet eyes staring back. My ivory skin no longer bore the signs of my labor from the day. No matter how many hours I spent in the sun, my stubborn ivory skin refused to tan like the other villagers—a fact I secretly envied.

I combed my long, dark hair, knowing that when it dried, it would be a frizzy mess. There was no avoiding it.

I donned leather pants and a form-fitting top, carefully returning my new blade to its sheath. I grabbed my old bag and checked my meager coin purse. If we were meeting a traveler with books tonight, I was going to need them.

A knock came from the front door, and I could hear my grandmother answer. Through the walls, I heard Grandmother's sweet voice—no doubt delivering her usual threats to Maël. The sweet old lady had quite the bite—a blessing or curse, depending on who you asked.

"We're going to be late!" Maël called out as I emerged from the back of the cottage.

I rolled my eyes and shook my head as I embraced my grandmother goodbye. "I told you I could've met you at the gate."

"Then he would've been really late trying to find out where you wandered off to on your way there," Grandmother chuckled. studied us with an odd hesitation. She grabbed my hand and spoke low, "Be careful, Alora. I love you as much as there are stars in our sky."

Something in her tone had shifted, so I gave her a reassuring smile and squeezed her tiny hand. "I love you as much as there are stars in our sky too. Thank you again for the blade."

She smiled softly and nodded, looking back at Maël, who shifted awkwardly, trying to grant us privacy. "You two better go." She shooed us out the door, and Maël led us through the village to the main gate. The wooden pillars might not match the grand gates in my beloved stories, but they meant home.

"Eleni threatened my manhood if I don't bring you home by dawn," Maël chuckled. "Try not to wander off tonight, I'd like to keep myself intact." He nudged me with his shoulder, almost pushing me into the bushes as we walked into the woods. I stumbled, struggling to catch my footing, but somehow righted myself. I pushed him sideways, paying him back in kind, barely disrupting his steady steps.

I flashed him a sly smile and batted my eyelashes at him, "I'll try, but it may be difficult. I'm sure you could manage if worst comes to worst."

His laugh rang through the darkness, the sound echoing through the trees, drawing an unbidden smile to my lips. My heart performed its usual treacherous dance and forced my thoughts back in line. We were just friends—that's all he wanted. And I would learn to be content with that.

CHAPTER 7

Traversing the main trail in the woods for what felt like hours. We chatted about the things from the week, some village gossip, but truthfully that was fine with me. I was nervous, more nervous than I had any right to be, doing night watch with my best friend.

I caught myself wondering how soft his lips might be…

Fuck. Sure, he'd teased and flirted throughout the years, but he'd never once asked for anything more than friendship. He'd never looked at me the way he did the other village girls. They were all so beautiful and dainty, not the type to get their hands dirty fighting or tracking through the forest. I wouldn't be surprised if he became betrothed soon. Perhaps to Lydia—all honey-gold hair and sky-blue eyes—or Alice, with her kind heart and chocolate curls framing rich ebony skin. Her family was well-respected within the community. She and Maël would make a beautiful couple. I would be happy for them, whoever he chose.

"Alora?" His voice startled me out of my inner thoughts. I snapped my head toward him, trying to figure out if he had said something I missed. He cleared his throat and gestured towards a spot on the soft ground, "did you want to take a break? We're about midway through."

I nodded and sat down on the ground near where he had pointed. He sat beside me and set his lantern between us. After rifling through his bag, he produced some packages.

I smiled. "Please thank your mom for me. She's the best cook in the village." I opened the cloth to find bread, cheese, and seasoned chicken. One bite of the chicken had me fighting back a moan.

He smiled between bites. ""I'll be sure to pass that along." We ate in comfortable silence until every morsel was gone.

The woods held their breath around us. From our spot in the small clearing, I could see stars winking through the canopy above—silent guardians watching over their watchers. The moonlight filtered through the leaves, casting dappled shadows that danced across the forest floor. The night air carried the sweet scent of wildflowers and earth, wrapping around us like a silk veil.

"Not quite what you had in mind for your birthday, huh?" Maël asked. When I turned to answer, I found him gazing at the stars. The lantern caught the gold in his eyes, making them gleam like honey. His brown hair was tousled as always—his mother's daily frustration, my secret delight. It suited him, wild and free. He caught me staring, and warmth bloomed in my cheeks.

"It's not," I said, "but I'd have only spent it with my grandmother before turning in. Besides, I love being in the woods, especially with a view like this." I gestured skyward. Maël kept his eyes on me as he nodded.

"Yeah, the view is breathtaking," he agreed.

His intense stare only deepened my blush. I glanced down, fidgeting with my sheath strap. "Did grandmother seem odd to you tonight?"

"When doesn't Eleni act odd?" He chuckled, probably thinking of all her peculiarities over the years. He had a point, but this was different.

"I mean weirder than usual," I explained. "She gave me my gift early—she always waits for my actual birthday. And when we left… her goodbye felt final."

"Don't people usually say goodbye when someone leaves? Maybe she was just excited about your gift?" he offered.

I considered for a moment. "Maybe. It's just unlike her. It didn't feel like her usual goodbye."

I felt Maël shift closer—or maybe that was just wishful thinking. "It's a big year," he said. "Most people get their powers at twenty-one. It changes things."

I nodded. He was right—it was nerve-wracking to wonder what might happen. Would I be a healer like her? Would flames dance at my fingertips, or would water bend to my will? Being fae, our senses and strength already bordered on godlike compared to humans. As a half-fae, Maël possessed keener senses than any human, but the elemental gifts had passed him by. Still, he'd never let that hold him back—something I'd always admired. Whenever I told him his real power was his endless optimism, he'd laugh and say optimism wouldn't stop a blade. So he trained, preparing for the day the war might reach our peaceful village. We'd been lucky so far, but luck was a fickle friend.

"Alora." *Gods, did he even know what my name on his tongue did to me?*

His hands fidgeted in the dirt as I met his intense gaze. As our eyes locked into each other, he swallowed, nervousness flickering across his features before vanishing like morning mist.

"I had another reason for asking you here tonight, beyond indulging your love of books."

"What better reason is there? Besides, Trenton bailed, remember?" I smiled, letting out a small laugh as he chuckled.

"For you? None. But I wasn't entirely honest earlier. Trenton didn't bail—I asked him to stay home so I could have you to myself."

I stayed silent as the air grew thick with anticipation. He pulled a small cloth from his pocket and offered it to me, "Happy Birthday, Alora."

With trembling fingers, I unwrapped the cloth. Inside lay a silver ring, its band adorned with delicate filigree—tiny flowers etched with impossible precision.

"Maël," I breathed, words failing me.

"I don't know what future you dream of—whether it's children, or finding some wealthy lord, or traveling to the biggest library in the realm to lose yourself in books forever. I know I'm not worthy of you. I've never been."

I stilled. *Was this really happening?* "But I can't imagine my life without you. Would you consider marrying me?"

I was utterly stunned. Since when had he ever considered marrying me? Why would he consider marrying me? No one wanted a wife who could gut a deer or fight like a man. Am I imagining this? He looked at me with so much hope in his eyes. I swallowed, feeling my voice tremble as I tried to reign in my racing thoughts and racing heart.

"Maël, I didn't think you thought of me like this. I always thought you'd ask Alice or Lydia, aren't they better matches for you?"

Maël gently shook his head as he reached for my hand, "I've always wanted it to be you. Lydia and Alice are nice, but they're not you. I've tried to tell you my feelings but every time all I could think about was that you probably didn't want to settle for half fae like me. I was worried I'd have to find a new sparring buddy if you rejected me."

I could feel tears start welling in my eyes. "What if I want to explore and hole myself up in some library and never come out?"

"Then I'll follow you and bring you meals and listen as you tell me about all of the books you've read." He smiled as he began to stand, guiding me up with him. His hands never leaving my own. "Whatever life it is you decide, if you'll have me, I'll follow you wherever that leads."

My heart couldn't take it anymore. In one swift motion, I wrapped my arms around his neck and crashed my lips against his. His mouth was as soft as I'd imagined, and the way he kissed me back had me melting into his arms. I pulled back for just a moment, my breath catching in my throat. "I will," I whispered, my voice thick with emotion. "I would love to marry you."

CHAPTER 8

Our shift melted into a haze of blissful moments. We stole furtive kisses, our laughter muffled by the rustling leaves.

Grandmother knew of his intentions—a realization that soothed my racing heart. Her uncharacteristic silence earlier made sense now; she'd never been one to keep secrets easily.

I couldn't believe that he had felt for me all that I had felt for him. The weight of years spent fearing he'd pledge himself to another lifted from my shoulders.

As dawn approached and our shift neared its end, we made our way toward the merchants' camp.

"Are you sure you want to tie yourself to me?" Maël teased, his eyes dancing with mischief. "Just because you're my wife, doesn't mean I'll stop teasing you or ease up on you with training."

A chuckle escaped me as I let go of his hand to give him a little shove. "I wouldn't have it any other way. But I'm not your wife yet, at least not until our ceremony."

"I hear spring is the ideal time," he mused, his voice dropping to a husky whisper, "though I'm not sure my patience will last that long." He pulled me close, wrapping one arm around my lower back, the other caressing my cheek. His breath ghosted across my skin as his lips traced a path of gentle kisses along my neck.

"I think I would prefer the fall time," I said breathlessly.

He pulled back, his eyes narrowed. "That's even further away."

Heat crept into my cheeks. "Well, fall would come before spring, but if that's too soon... I just always thought fall was prettier than spring."

A slow smile spread across his face, lighting up his eyes. "This fall sounds perfect, Lor. I'd marry you tomorrow if you'd let me. I've waited twenty-one years to call you mine. I won't wait a day longer than necessary."

I stood on my tiptoes to place a soft kiss on his cheek. "A fall wedding it is."

As we approached the encampment, an eerie silence settled over the woods. The merchant tents emerged from the tree line, but something was wrong—no one was there.

Maël's voice echoed through the clearing as he called out, but only silence answered. He knelt by the fire while I approached the nearest tent. "This was put out not too long ago," he said, his voice tight with concern. He noted how unusual it was for the merchants to leave their site completely unattended.

I approached a tent only to find a bedroll inside. I hurriedly looked into a second tent, my hand hovering over my dagger's hilt . As I lifted the flap, my breath caught in my throat. Metal gleamed in the dark. I opened the tent flaps wider to reveal the horrifying contents: an iron cage, cruel shackles, and other sinister implements I'd never seen a merchant carry.

"Maël," I called in a hushed whisper, feeling a pit grow in my stomach. He rushed over and looked inside the tent, his hand on the hilt of his sword.

"Gods," he turned toward me, the color draining from his face. "We need to go and alert the village before whoever set up this camp returns."

The truth felt heavy as it sank in—these weren't merchants at all.

CHAPTER 9

e ran through the woods, Maël leading me through a shortcut that avoided the main road. We needed to get home fast and couldn't find the owners of the camp along the road. As we neared the village, more light peered through the trees. The sun was still rising, casting an eerie glow through the canopy.

Breaking through the dense foliage, bodies strewn across blood-soaked grass, I finally understood why, my heart dropping like a stone as I saw the front gate ablaze, the wood crackling against orange flames. The entire village was engulfed in a hellish inferno.

"Find whoever you can and hide in the woods," Maël commanded, drawing his sword from its scabbard. "Whatever happens, get to safety, I will find you after." I met his gaze and nodded, swallowing hard.

I drew my dagger as I followed him into the chaos-stricken village. People were running, screaming. Dark armored figures cut down villagers indiscriminately, their blades flashing in the firelight. Maël clashed with one as I darted towards some of the homes not completely engulfed in flames, desperate to save anyone I could.

Inside, I found only the dead—faces I'd known all my life, now empty vessels staring into nothing.

As I emerged from the last house I'd searched, I saw a child cowering by a crate. Barely old enough to count his summers, I ran towards him, keeping my eyes peeled for any of the attackers.

"Hey, are you okay? Let's get you somewhere safe." I reached out my hand. The child's face, pale beneath the soot and tear tracks, bobbed in a solemn nod as he grabbed my hand.

"My mommy wouldn't wake up."

My heart splintered, and I guided us through the maze of burning homes towards a dense copse of trees. I glanced around and motioned for him to hide there. "Keep your head down, I'll come back for you. If you see any of the bad men, run into the woods and don't stop, okay?" He nodded. That was good enough for me, and I prayed none of the attackers ventured this way.

I ran back towards the smoldering ruins of our once peaceful village. Recognizing the path to our home, I pushed my legs harder, my lungs burning from the smoke. I could hear the shouts of men amidst the thick haze of smoke, but I couldn't hear the screams of villagers. I refused to contemplate the meaning behind that silence. That silence held more horror than a thousand screams.

As I ROUNDED THE CORNER, my grandmother's screams pierced the air. Our cottage blazed, a fierce orange inferno consuming my grandmother's beloved garden. She stood among the wreckage, a vision of spiteful hate.

"Oi, is this the one?" One of the brutes surrounding her growled to another. The commander stood taller and appeared to hold the authority.

"Aye, that's her. You've made some powerful enemies, old woman. Took us a while to track you down." He sneered, his lips curling with malice. In one swift, merciless motion, he thrust his sword into her chest.

A scream tore from my throat as my grandmother crumpled to the ground. I was mere steps away but not close enough. My heart shattered into a thousand pieces as I watched the life drain from her eyes. In a blur of rage and desperation, I unsheathed my dagger and buried it in the nearest man's flesh. He didn't even have time to register what was happening, his words lost in a wet, gurgling gasp. I whirled on the others, there were two more and their leader. They eyed me with amusement, their laughter a cruel taunt. I was alone, it was clear they had razed the entire village. I just hoped Maël had escaped, that he was somewhere safe, helping others hide.

"What do we have here?" The leader smirked. "Care to warm my tent, lovely?" His cronies chuckled as he took a measured step forward.

"I'd sooner slit my own throat," I snarled, inching towards my fallen grandmother. Maybe I could heal her, maybe it wasn't too late.

"That can be arranged," the leader stated coldly, nodding to the brute on his right.

"What kind of blade is this?" The brute I'd fought asked, stooping to retrieve my fallen dagger. It sparkled like starlight despite the blood now flecking its surface. The leader glanced at it, and his face drained of color as he looked then to me. His demeanor changed instantly, like he felt threatened.

"Kill her now. We can't risk her surviving," he commanded.

I tried to get away, but I was only mere steps away from my attacker, his sword poised to strike. I scrambled, reaching with my good arm for another weapon when my eyes caught movement past the man stalking towards me.

Maël fought another man, he had the leverage. He swiftly gutted his opponent and caught sight of me as the man fell. Fear laced his eyes as he realized what was happening. "ALORA!" He called. Whatever he was going to say next was cut short.

Gods, please, I begged. *Anyone but him, take me in his place, just let him live.*

A blade protruded from his abdomen, shock etched across his face as he fell to his knees, his eyes fixed on me, filled with sorrow.

"That's the last one, Captain Johan," Maël's murderer called out triumphantly.

I couldn't see how near my own soon-to-be killer was, time slowed as my eyes stayed on that same spot. On the man laying dead on the ground. My grandmother not far, struck down. That was the last one. It was only me, no one else to save our village, no one left to defend. I felt a sudden rush of warmth yet coolness as I cried out, something foreign erupting from within. My body trembled as my power burst forth, surrounding us in darkness. I could see the men looking around uncertain, as if they couldn't see. I took the chance to launch myself at the one before me, twisting his sword straight into his own neck. Distracted by the lack of sight, he didn't have a chance to react as I took his life. I kept hold of the sword and kicked his body off it, it landed with a sick thud. I could barely stand as I looked at the remaining three. Warmth bloomed in my hand, I looked down to find a pure light flame licking my fingertips.

"What the fuck are you?" The leader gasped, his eyes trained on my hand, the only light in this darkness. His blade poised.

I could feel the power building, I couldn't control it. It was coming no matter what I did. I cried out, trying to will my body under control. It was too much. Flames surrounded me, my flames. Pure white, growing higher and faster. I could hear the leader shout something but I couldn't make it out, barely conscious in my own body as power flooded me and unleashed itself upon the world.

Let it, I told myself. *Let it cleanse the world.*

CHAPTER 10

I awoke to a world of ash, the remnants of my community and their homes reduced to nothing but dust and memories. The darkness I had summoned and the flames I had unleashed had vanished, leaving only destruction in their wake.

I searched where my grandmother had once laid but found nothing but scattered ashes. I knelt beside them, cries of anguish ringing in the silent space. The woman who raised me, taught me everything I knew, was gone. I had no parents—my mother lost, my father presumed dead, a ghost never mentioned.

I love you as much as there are stars in our sky.

I stood and glanced at the spot where I last saw Maël, finding a hollow relief in knowing he was gone before my flames could consume him. My heart shattered as I thought of the boy I knew, the man I had loved even when I didn't think he loved me back. I touched the ring he gave me, a promise now broken.

I stumbled through the ash-covered ruins to the cluster of trees where I'd left the young boy, only to find more desolation. Maybe he got away before the flames came. I searched the tree line to no avail. There were no survivors other than me. If this could be called survival, I was tired, bloodied, and if I didn't find something for this wound on my arm soon it would fester.

I sifted through the wreckage, my fingers coated in ash, desperate for anything salvageable. I cursed, what was I supposed to do now? I kept walking until I caught something glinting in the dying sunlight. As I reached down to pick it up my heartache grew. It was the last thing my grandmother ever gave me, my dagger of starlight.

I used the blade to cut a strip from my shirt and bound it around my arm. I may not have healing magic, but I picked up some basics when I could. I put the dagger in its sheath and held the sword I had used to slay the fae who came here. Their camp, with its promise of provisions, lay not far from here. With nothing left in this wasteland, it was my only hope. Assuming they hadn't escaped my flames, their remains now indistinguishable from the ash around me.

I trudged towards the encampment, my steps faltering as I passed through the skeletal remains of the village gate. The once-welcoming structures were now nothing but memories, their warmth replaced by the chill of desolation.

As I pressed on towards the promise of survival, a part of me longed for Death's embrace, a twisted solace in this wasteland of ash and regret.

Darkness had swallowed the woods whole by the time I stumbled upon what I prayed was the camp.

The clearing looked vaguely familiar, the fire pit a ghostly reminder of my last moments with Maël. It was the only sign someone had ever occupied the space.

The iron cages, bedrolls, and every trace of the murderers who'd brought death to my village had vanished. Someone had survived the chaos, but who? It couldn't have been just one man. Even two fae males would've struggled with those iron cages.

The three mercenaries I'd faced outside our cottage burned in my memory like a brand. They'd stolen the two people I loved most in this world from me forever. I clenched my fists, feeling the shadows pulse around me, thirsting for retribution.

I slumped onto a weathered log by the long-forgotten pit, my fingers seeking out the hilt of my dagger—one of the last remnants of my life before. The weight of it in my palm was a cold comfort. I couldn't yield to Death's seductive whisper, couldn't surrender to the temptation of joining my loved ones in the great beyond. No, that wasn't my fate, at least, not yet.

I traced the edge of the blade with my finger, watching as starlight kissed its surface like scattered diamonds. The eerie quiet of the woods pressed in around me, but it didn't unnerve me. It couldn't. I knew in my bones that I would meet Death again, like an old friend. Next time, I wouldn't greet Death as its victim, I would be its harbinger.

Live your life, Lor. Let me go and live.

The grief clawed at my chest, threatening to tear me apart. Maël's voice echoed in my mind, as real as if he were right beside me, close enough to touch.

"I won't rest until I find them," I whispered to the darkness, each word a blade against my throat. "I will harvest their souls like they've reaped so many others." The words branded themselves into my soul, a blood oath I couldn't break.

The dagger bit deeper into my palm as my fingers clenched, blood welling around the blade. They had taken everything from me, yet never imagined what would rise from the ashes of their destruction. I would become their reckoning, a nightmare forged in the crucible of their own cruelty. And I wouldn't rest until vengeance was mine.

CHAPTER II

One Year Later...

I sat on the rooftop in Oakston, a city of Esmeray, my gaze fixed upon the home ahead, waiting for my mark. It had taken a year to find the trail of one of the survivors—Archie, the one who had wanted to "have his fun" with me back at the camp. I had tracked him for nearly a month, learning his habits, and with midnight nearing, I knew it wouldn't be long until his drunken self stumbled home.

This past year hadn't been easy.

Haunted by a shattered heart, I had barely managed to drag myself from The Great Woods, finding refuge in a remote township within Esmeray. Though some kind souls tended to my wounds, the shadow of war had left the town a hollow shell of what it once was. Despite my gratitude, I pressed forward, surviving on what I could hunt and earn, haunting taverns by night in search of any whisper that might lead me to the men who ruined my life.

Gradually, I learned to embrace my newfound power. What I had first thought was darkness turned out to be shadows. In the depths of the woods, I honed my craft, learning to bend shadows to my will, pulling them from trees until they blanketed entire clearings.

I became one with the shadows, watching huntsmen pass mere inches from where I stood, their oblivious forms close enough to touch.

But the fire—the white flames—remained untouched, a power I dared not summon after what happened to the village.

The shadows proved useful enough, yet the memory of that strange, searing warmth that accompanied the white flames still haunted me.

To summon that power again would be to risk losing control entirely.

I had made a vow of vengeance, and I intended to keep it—even if it meant restraining the very power that burned within my blood.

It wasn't until a month ago that I happened upon a local tavern here where this drunkard bragged about what he'd seen in his travels, including hidden villages within the woods. When I caught sight of his face, time froze, my blood turning to ice. My fingers trembled against the wooden table, memories of that night crashing through me like a tidal wave of horror. It took all of my willpower not to slit his throat right there. When he finally had his fill of ale, he stumbled out of the tavern, and I slipped into the night behind him. Once outside, I used the shadows to conceal my steps, though the fool never even glanced back. That was the first night I tracked him to his home.

For weeks, I scouted the dilapidated home, learning his habits, where he frequented, and who visited.

I was frustrated to find his former companions never came by. The man lived a pathetic life, spending his days nursing hangovers and his nights drinking and entertaining paid company.

As I watched him stumble home night after night, my resolve only grew fiercer. Every stagger, every stumble was a reminder of the pain he'd caused, the lives he'd ruined. With each passing night, I felt the shadows within me grow deeper, more ravenous for the justice I was about to serve.

The night before last, he'd brought home a woman—human.

From my hiding spot, I'd winced as my fae hearing caught every sordid detail until the woman shrieked, cursed, and stormed out.

She'd spat something about inadequacies—whether his manhood or his coin purse was lacking, she'd wanted neither.

Tonight, blessed be the stars, he came home alone.

The shadows embraced me as I glided to the side of the house, peering through a window to find him nearly unconscious at the small table. I crept to the back, coaxing the window open with well-practiced fingers. Moonlight spilled across weathered floorboards, casting long shadows that danced at my command, while the musty scent of stale ale and unwashed linens assaulted my senses.

Through the ajar door, I spotted him slumped at the table, his shallow snores filling the silence.

I sighed. This couldn't be so easy. Silent as death, I positioned myself behind him, my presence a ghost.

He didn't deserve the mercy of dying in his sleep.

With my dagger ready in one hand, I seized the tankard and doused Archie with its contents.

I commanded the shadows away, unveiling myself.

His eyes locked onto me, nearly doubling in size.

"What in the hells?!" he bellowed, lurching to his feet.

I lunged forward, slamming him back into his seat, my dagger kissing his throat. "Remember me? You seemed so eager for my company before."

Archie's eyes darted wildly, his chest heaving as he gripped the edge of his chair. "That was before I knew what you were," he spat. "You're a monster. Nothing but destruction from the likes of you."

A cold laugh escaped my lips. "Oh, Archie," I purred. "The only ones who brought destruction were you and your crew." I pressed the dagger deeper, drawing a thin line of blood. "Where are they?" I demanded, my voice dropping to a dangerous whisper.

He winced, a bead of blood trailing down his neck. "Loose lips never got anyone nowhere," he growled, defiance flickering in his eyes.

"Wrong answer," I sighed, my voice ice. "But I guess I'll just have to hunt them down like I did you. Like you did to all of them." The blade sang across his throat. His eyes went wild, thick fingers scrabbling at the gushing wound.

I watched the light fade from his eyes, victory and emptiness warring in my chest. "They'll... kill... you..." he choked out, his words dissolving into a wet gurgle as the life drained from him. His eyes rolled back, and he slumped forward, dead. I remained still, the hollow victory tasting like ash in my mouth.

The silence shattered with measured applause.

I whirled around, my heart leaping into my throat. A tall, lithe figure lounged in the doorway, shrouded in shadow.

Wrapped in black leather, they radiated power that felt wrong— neither fae nor human. Their face covered beneath a dark cloak.

"It's not often someone gets to my mark before I do," the figure mused as they stepped closer to our dearly departed friend. "Who sent you?"

I shifted, my grip on the dagger white-knuckled. "No one sent me," I said, my voice steadier than I felt. Every instinct screamed at me to flee. As the stranger advanced, I retreated, my eyes darting to the bedroom behind me. If I could make it to the window...

"Are you a free agent?" they inquired, halting just out of arm's reach, their head tilted in curiosity.

"I'm merely someone with a grudge," I retorted, struggling to keep the tremor from my voice. "I didn't mean to take your mark. By all means, tell your employer you did it. I got what I needed from this."

"If you decide you need employment, find me at the tavern in

Bridgedale, just over the Sunnevan border. Ask the barkeep about vengeance." They made a lazy circular gesture with their hand. "Judging by that exchange with old Archie here, I'm sure that won't be difficult for you." They melted into the shadows like ink into water. I didn't hesitate, launching myself through the room and out the window, the night swallowing me whole.

ARCHIE'S DEATH brought little comfort. He was just one of three who had devastated our village. I wandered through the town's narrow streets, my feet carrying me towards its outskirts. My chest felt hollow, each breath a reminder of all I'd lost as empty buildings stared back at me with shattered windows like accusing eyes. There was nothing left for me here.

Could I become a blade for hire? My stomach churned at the thought, but survival had a way of reshaping morals into mere suggestions. A hollow ache in my belly reminded me of more pressing concerns. I hadn't seen any signs of deer since the woods near the last city, and between here and Sunneva, nothing but war-ravaged territory. My coin purse was meager—I could maybe afford some bread whenever I found the next trader, but I'd have to find a way to earn more after.

The stars only twinkled mockingly at my perpetual state of being lost. I was always lost.

Another pang of hunger twisted my insides. I drew my bow, keeping my eyes peeled for any sign of a small animal I could roast. I didn't dare travel beyond the path. My inner compass spun wildly, and I feared straying from the path would leave me truly adrift. A slight rustling caught my attention. I crouched, pulling shadows to me as I crept towards the bush when a squirrel popped out. It wasn't a deer, but it'd do.

The squirrel fell to my arrow, and I built a small fire near the path. The trail remained visible, a lifeline I dared not abandon in search of water. I made short work of cooking the meat and said a small prayer, thankful to not starve tonight. I watched the flames dance, sparks rising when the wood crackled. Suddenly, the gentle flames transformed into a searing inferno, devouring my village in my mind's eye. I winced, never again. I wouldn't release that destruction ever again.

I laid beneath the stars, with only the warmth of the fire to comfort me. Memories of Maël flooded my thoughts, bittersweet and piercing. What would he think of the path I now walked? Would he understand my need to rid the world of such evil? Would he still want me if he knew I was considering becoming an assassin? Part of me wanted to believe he would, saying something about living honorably. But deep down, I knew different—when he proposed, he would have moved heaven and hell for us, despite my doubts about our chances. He would've understood doing something bad with good intentions, and he would've been excited for an adventure. I twirled the silver ring around my finger. Perhaps embracing this new path, this adventure, wasn't such a terrible idea—at least until I could reunite with my people.

CHAPTER 12

Cursing under my breath, I hauled my freshly killed buck behind me, my boots struggling for purchase with each labored step. The carcass dragged at my aching muscles as the metallic scent of blood filled the air. Sweat trickled down my spine, dark strands of hair plastered to my face as I forced myself onward.

After days of searching for civilization, my heart sank at the sight of the town before me. Fear and exhaustion coiled in my gut, like a serpent waiting to strike.

Sunneva's forces had clearly claimed this town as their own. The buildings near the entrance lay broken, reduced to mounds of splintered wood and shattered stone. Wooden spikes jutted from the walls like teeth, each one a trophy of Sunneva's conquest.

The Sunnevan guards at the gate barely spared a glance at me and my quarry.

You needed to bag a large one to have a chance to get the supplies you need, Maël murmured in my mind.

My heart stuttered, a mixture of comfort and pain washing over me at the sound of his voice.

I grunt, struggling to breathe as I continued to drag the large beast. *I should've listened to you more when we were training.*

You're doing fine, just a few more steps, Lor. His presence faded like mist at dawn, retreating to that dark corner of my mind where my sanity comes into question. The loss of his voice, whether real or imagined, left an ache in my chest.

I approached the blacksmith's forge, my gaze lingered on the arrows on display. These arrows put my old ones to shame. My chest tightened at the thought and I shove the feeling away. No use dwelling on memories of home, especially not over arrows.

The blacksmith looked up from the sword he was hammering on the anvil. The burly man's eyes widened as they landed on the buck I'd dragged behind me. The muscles in his arms tensed as he paused his work, sweat gleaming on his brow.

"That's quite the kill you've got there, miss," he said, setting the iron weapon down and wiping his hands on a grimy rag.

I nodded, fighting to keep my expression neutral despite my exhaustion. My fingers flexed against the rope, refusing to show weakness.

He chuckled, the sound rumbling like distant thunder.

"I'd say so. You looking to trade?"

"Arrows," I said, jerking my chin toward the display. "And I need my bow repaired."

The blacksmith's gaze sharpened, sizing me up like a weapon he meant to forge.

"Let's see that bow of yours, then."

I carefully unstrapped it from my back, mindful to keep my cloak in place. The less attention I drew, the better. The bow barely held through this last hunt—its string frayed and the wood chipped and worn.

He took it, turning it over in his calloused hands. "This has seen better days. But it's good craftsmanship. I can fix it up for you."

I nodded, my eyes drawn inexorably to the arrows again.

"Depends on how many you want," he said, following my gaze. "That buck of yours could fetch a fair amount."

I stepped closer, keeping my voice low. "How about we make a deal? The meat for the arrows and the bow repair."

The blacksmith's eyebrows shot up. "That's quite the offer, miss, but it's too much. I'll replace your bow and fill your quiver. Deal?"

"Deal," I said, my violet eyes meeting his. I could see the curiosity there, the questions he yearned to ask but wouldn't.

He hesitated, then nodded. "Alright. You've got yourself a deal."

As he turned to gather the arrows, I caught sight of my reflection in a polished shield. My face was gaunt, my eyes haunted. I barely recognized myself anymore.

You're doing what needs to be done, Maël's voice whispers in my mind.

I closed my eyes, willing the phantom voice away. When I opened them again, the blacksmith was back, arrows in hand.

"These should do you nicely," he said, holding them out.

I took them, testing their weight and balance. They were not perfect, but they'll do. "Thank you," I murmured.

He nodded, already turning his attention to my bow. "I've got some bows close to this size in the back." He gestured towards a back door, "Give me just a moment."

I nodded, slipping the arrows into my quiver. As he turned, a scream erupted from a yard away.

I whipped around, my hand instinctively reaching for my dagger. A Sunnevan guard's angry shouts sliced through the buzzing market, a young woman struggling against his iron-tight grip. Tears streamed down her face as she twisted and turned, her hand pushing on his trying to break free.

"Please, let me go!" she pleaded, her voice cracking with fear. "Papa!"

The guard's face twisted with rage. "Shut up and come with me, no one's going to save you."

My breath hitched as I watched the scene unfold. The woman's desperate cries for help tugged at something I've pushed deep inside me, a part I wished had died along with my village. Every instinct screamed at me to intervene, but drawing attention to myself could be fatal. My stomach churned with the weight of my choices, duty warring against conscience with every beat of my heart.

Could you forgive yourself for walking away? Maël's voice whispered in my mind. My heart shattered at the weight of his words, each syllable a blade against my conscience.

I drew a deep breath, my decision crystallizing like frost on glass.

The shadows answered my call, wrapping around me like a lover's embrace, familiar and cold. The market's sounds faded to a dull hum as I moved closer to the altercation, keeping my steps on dryer ground to avoid slipping in the mud.

The guard dragged the woman towards an alley, his fingers dug into her arm hard enough to leave bruises. She stumbled, nearly falling, and he yanked her upright with a snarl.

"Papa, help me! Someone, anyone, please!" she cried out, her wild hair whipping around her face as she fought against the guard's grip. But the townspeople kept their heads down, pretending not to see.

I slipped between two market stalls, my shadows coiling around me as I prepared to jump guard from behind. Anxiety coiled in my chest, but my hands remained steady as I drew my dagger.

Be careful, Lor, Maël's voice whispered. *You don't know what you're getting into.*

I ignored him and focused on the guard and the terrified woman. I wouldn't stand by and watch another innocent suffer.

The moment presented itself when she slipped, her knees hitting the mud and almost taking her attacker down with her. I struck, my shadows surging forward as I crashed into the struggling pair, breaking his hold on her.

His face contorted into a sneer before his eyes found me, fear bleeding into them as he took me in. A creature of darkness instead of a mere girl.

He fell, scrambling backwards as I took measured steps towards him. My dagger melded with the rest of me as I stalked my prey.

"Please, please," he begged, his voice trembling, "I-I let her go, see? Please don't take me." He backed himself into a wall, silence falling over the market as the townsfolk watched the sight. Even the other Sunnevan guards stayed back in fear of what they were witnessing.

I stopped beside him, crouching down to meet his gaze. Could he see past the void where my eyes should be? I tilted my head to the side as I studied the man. He's human, built with large muscles and clearly compensating. I turned my head to the side and saw the woman now hiding behind the blacksmith, who stood protectively before her, eyes unblinking and ready for a brawl. Now that I saw them side by side, he must be the father she'd called for.

"Not willingly," I pointed out. The acrid scent of urine filled the air. "Would you have beaten her? Raped her? Forced her upon all of your buddies to wet your tiny cocks?" With each question my shadows writhed with my growing rage.

He furiously shook his head, "N-no, I would never—"

"Yes, you would." I snarled, my blade flashing out to silence his lies forever. I rose, my gaze sweeping over the guards watching in horror as their friend's life ebbed away. "Who's next?" I challenged, shadows writhing around me.

The guards scattered like leaves in a storm, their courage crumbling before the darkness that consumed me. Typical Sunnevans—always choosing self-preservation over honor.

I glided back to the forge, lifting the new bow from the counter. The heavy presence of the blacksmith loomed behind me as I tested the length and weight of the new gear.

"Thank you, my daughter—" His voice broke with emotion, "she is the only family I have left. That bow is not enough of a payment for what you did."

I slung the bow onto my back and turned to face the man. Sheltered from the prying eyes of the community, I released my shadows, allowing him to see me clearly. "This war has already taken enough from everyone. I won't accept payment for defending an innocent." I took a step past him but he thrust a meaty hand out.

"Wait," he hurried to a tall shelf, bringing down a short black roll of cloth, "these are my finest daggers. Obsidian from the mage's mountain, please take them." He presented the bundle to me, and I accepted it with hesitation. I examined one of the blades, its deep black surface gleaming as it settled perfectly in my hands. "May they keep you safe in your travels."

I inclined my head in thanks and slipped out the back of the forge. Whispers of "Death's Wraith" rippled amongst the people around me, my new daggers a comforting weight against my body.

The assassin could lead me to Johan—the monster who had razed my village and stolen Maël from me. My heart clenched at the thought of him, but I pushed the pain aside. There's no room for weakness now.

You're getting close, Maël's voice echoed in my mind. A constant reminder of my lost love. *Be careful, Lor.*

"I know," I muttered to myself.

The town fell away behind me as I melted into the forest's embrace. Each life I took added another weight to my conscience, another shadow to my soul. The whispers of "Death's Wraith" followed me like a curse, but the memory of that girl's relieved face made it bearable. I'd chosen this path—becoming the monster they feared to protect those who couldn't protect themselves. At least Maël's voice, whether phantom or memory, anchored me to who I once was. That innocent girl who dreamed of more than vengeance was gone, transformed by necessity into something darker, deadlier.

As the shadows welcomed me home, I could only pray that somewhere, somehow, Maël would understand what I'd become.

CHAPTER 13

I reached Bridgedale with minimal trouble. Okay, I got turned around a couple of times, but some nice merchants helped me right myself. My days were consumed by endless riding, while nights were spent foraging and reading by firelight. The solitary book in my possession made me ache for my modest library back home. I couldn't reasonably ask the merchants if they had one for sale—I needed to conserve my coin for what lay ahead.

After crossing over the border of Sunneva, I realized two things. First, Sunneva's obsession with solar imagery was suffocating. Phrases like "Sunneva, Kingdom of the Sun," "Blessed by the Sun," and "Sun Blessed" were everywhere. This tiny town was practically drowning in brilliant golden orbs with dazzling rays in all styles. I shuddered to think what the capital might look like. The thought of a sun-shaped capital with a golden castle made me chuckle despite myself.

Second, I noticed that Sunneva's fortunes were significantly better than Esmeray's. My experience of Esmeray was limited to the small settlements bordering the woods, which marked the boundary between the two kingdoms, but the contrast was already apparent.

Esmeray's towns were modest, with surrounding areas bearing scars of destruction. Blackened ruins dotted the landscape like festering wounds, while broken fences and abandoned fields told stories of lives hastily abandoned. Some villages near the woods had been entirely wiped out by the war, leaving the inhabitants weary but clinging to hope for an end to the conflict. This Sunnevan town appeared marginally better off, with most of the surrounding farmland relatively unscathed. Shop signs had faded under the relentless sun. Ironically, the only elements untouched by this dullness were the golden sun emblems plastered across the streets, benches, fountains, and bridges. They gleamed with a golden radiance, a constant reminder of the symbol they embodied.

I pressed on along the path as the sun began its descent. Golden light bathed the town square in a hazy glow. I spotted a baker's stall getting ready to pack up for the day. My stomach growled at the sight of a solitary muffin on display. The baker regarded me with an impatient arch of his brow, clearly wanting to finish cleaning up and close shop for the day.

Rummaging in my pocket for coins, I asked, "What's the price for that muffin?"

"Two silvers," the man replied curtly. He watched me count out the coins onto his stall, arms crossed. He gave me a solemn nod in acceptance.

I grabbed the muffin and surveyed the square. "Any recommendations for a good ale around here?"

He pointed down a distant road. "The Sunlit Tankard's down that way. It's a bit rough, but they'll leave you be if you don't cause trouble." The baker wiped his hands on his flour-dusted apron and lowered his voice. "Mind the regulars near the back wall—they're fond of their dice games and don't take kindly to strangers watching too close." He gathered his remaining wares, that warning hanging in the air.

While the sun's rays still painted the sky, I searched for a vantage point near the tavern's alley to observe my contact's arrival before our meeting. I found a sturdy crate wedged between two buildings, perfectly positioned to give me a clear view of the tavern's entrance. Keeping to the shadows, I summoned the darkness, concealing myself as I settled onto the crate. From this hidden vantage point, I watched the tavern while forcing down the disappointingly bland muffin. The dense, dry crumbs felt like sawdust in my mouth, each bite more tasteless than the last. The alley stayed quiet at first. As twilight deepened, patrons began trickling in. The crowd filtered through—working girls, off-duty guards, the occasional rough sort, but no one with my target's distinctive gait appeared.

As darkness claimed the sky, I rose and stretched, attempting to calm the nervous fluttering in my stomach. Approaching the door, I let the darkness fall away, bracing myself for whatever lay beyond. The sharp tang of stale ale and pipe smoke drifted through the weathered door, mingling with bursts of raucous laughter from within.

CHAPTER 14

My gaze swept across the tavern, taking in the sight of long wooden tables filled with a diverse crowd. Soldiers shared ales after a grueling day, their armor emblazoned with the blessed sun, while courtesans from the local brothel wove between tables, their artfully styled hair catching the lamplight.

My fingers absently traced the ends of my dark hair. Despite my own reluctance to use feminine charms, I couldn't help but admire their grace—even if I could barely manage a simple braid.

Before that night with Maël, I'd never given much thought to my own appeal. My heart ached thinking of him. His training-tousled hair, the way his muscles moved beneath sun-kissed skin—everything about him seemed to call to my touch. All this time, I'd believed he was destined for another, when in truth, those captivating smiles were meant for me alone. He was truly mine in every way that I was his. Time lost to silence and misunderstanding, our future ripped away before we could claim it.

I thumbed the ring around my neck as I approached the bar. A burly man lumbered over, his expression suggesting I was already trying his patience. I lifted my chin, determined not to show any sign of weakness.

"I-", I didn't even get to finish as he grunted and dropped a key in front of me.

"Second door on ye right, I wouldn't keep 'em waiting if I were you," he said gruffly, already turning away to tend to his other patrons.

His demeanor brought Geralt to mind—all growl and no grace. I sighed as I took the key from the counter and headed towards the staircase. I paused at the door, noting the empty hallway and the unusual silence. The lamplight cast shadows in the hall, and I fought the urge to draw them to me, to hide me from what awaited inside. But they'd already witnessed my shadow tricks—there would be no easy deception tonight.

I slipped the key into the lock and turned it. The door swung inward to expose a dimly lit chamber, illuminated only by a crackling fireplace. The room held little: a small bed hugged the far wall, while two wingback chairs faced the hearth.

In one chair lounged a figure with fluid elegance, their limbs arranged with calculated indifference. They observed me with undisguised interest, shadows dancing across the hood they wore.

"I almost thought you wouldn't show," they drawled, voice dripping with equal parts arrogance and indifference. I approached, they remained perfectly still, studying my every movement.

Despite my unease, I masked my discomfort with a nonchalant shrug, sinking into the other chair with feigned casualness. "To be fair, I never promised my presence."

They chuckled, straightening. "But you are indeed here. Have you considered my offer?"

"Remind me, what exactly are you offering?"

They leaned forward, pushing back their hood to reveal hair like spun candlelight, blue eyes gleaming with predatory interest and lips curved in a savage smile. "I'm offering you exactly what you seek, little one—vengeance."

I met her eyes, weighing my response. Had I been so transparent with my purpose?

"I'm only guessing," she said, leaning back to watch the flames devour the log inside.

"You're no trained assassin, yet I watched you murder Archie. I collected that bounty myself, so I know you weren't on contract. You have a score to settle—and clearly, you're not finished yet."

Her gaze found mine, calculating, weighing my worth like a merchant appraising rare goods.

"I'll train you. You'll take the jobs I assign. In return—shelter, meals, payment for your work, and my help finding whoever you're hunting."

There it was—the choice I'd wrestled with since learning of this place.

The resources I desperately needed, paid for in blood.

Could I do this? I studied her face, searching for... something.

Her feral smile softened into something familiar—a fierce determination that burned as bright as the flames behind her.

I knew that look—it was the same fire that had driven me as I hunted my village's murderers.

I nodded once. "I accept. Who are you?"

She tossed a coin purse into my lap. "Vanya. That's your cut from Archie. Now come—your training begins."

A chill traced my spine as I rose to follow her. I was stepping into a world of shadows and blood, but beneath my fear, hope flickered to life. Vengeance was finally within reach, and I would pay whatever price it demanded.

CHAPTER 15

Vanya drew the hood of her midnight cloak over her head, gesturing for me to follow suit. My worn cloak was nothing like her opulent one, the threadbare hood refusing to stay in place even in the gentlest wind.

Drawing on my power, I pulled the hood up and coaxed the shadows to me, weaving them around my neck and lower face like a living, breathing cowl. Vanya's eyes glittered with interest as she turned to lead the way.

I followed my new mentor out of the little tavern, slipping out through a window. Our fingers found purchase on the wall like water flowing upward, our feet finding holds in the weathered bricks. In a heartbeat, we were atop the roof, leaping to the next with silent grace, our movements fluid as shadows dancing across moonlit stone.

Like whispers in the night, we ghosted as we made our way across town. Or so I hoped. The assassin could very well be leading me into a trap, and I would have to guess which direction was the exit. I tried memorizing our route, but after our third turn, I couldn't tell if we were moving East of the tavern or West. Every so often I would find a wet patch, my worn boots threatening to slip. I felt out of my element. What in the gods' names had I agreed to?

Vanya moved fearlessly with the grace of a cat, ready to strike her target. I, on the other hand, was like a fawn learning to walk, clinging to my newfound powers like a drowning sailor to driftwood. I shook my head, cleared my thoughts, and focused on the moment at hand. I could do this. This was how I would find the last man and rid this land of his evil.

Vanya crouched ahead. I crept behind her and mirrored the movement, scanning the silent streets and shadowed homes, desperate to catch a glimpse of whatever had caught her attention.

"Look there," she pointed towards a three-story structure, shadowed between two others down the road. The building loomed dark and foreboding, its weathered facade a testament to countless secrets. "That's the target. Towards the top window, there is an office of a man who has found himself on someone's list. Get in. Be discreet —they will alert the whole block you're there if they sense a threat. Kill him and get out."

I realized there was no "we" in that. This was my test.

I swallowed. "And if I get caught?"

Vanya gave me a predator's smile, "You'd be better off slitting your own throat. Don't get caught." I nodded, and she sat back on the roof, content to watch the spectacle unfold from her lofty perch.

I took a deep breath before I closed my eyes and pulled more shadows to me until I all but disappeared. Here on the roof, there was nothing above me to provide any coverage to make me completely disappear. Like death's own wraith, I imagined I must have looked like a nightmare given form, a creature born of shadow and starless night.

I stepped to the edge of our perch and started to slowly climb my way down, my fingers biting into the harsh brick of windowsills until I dropped onto the one below. Climbing trees with Maël when we were younger never served me so well.

Once I finally reached the ground, I was nearly invisible. Not a soul out at the hour, I cast a final glance in both directions before prowling over to the building Vanya had directed me to. It didn't seem unique, squat compared to its neighbors. The cobblestone of the street led up to simple stone steps that sat before a wooden door. As I drew closer, I noticed the door had an eye-level opening. Maybe this wasn't just someone's home.

Hearing laughter approaching, I melted into the shadows at the corner of the building, my fingers curling around the hilt of my dagger.

Taking stock of my surroundings, a man flanked by two women stumbled toward the entrance, their laughter betraying the slur of too much wine.

The viewing slot scraped open, though the door remained hidden from my view. The man murmured in hushed tones to the unseen guard until the snap of the latch echoed and they were granted passage. Perfect. More potential witnesses to complicate my mission.

Only after the viewing slot slammed shut and the lock clicked into place did I move.

The words became my prayer: *Get in. Kill the man. Get out. Don't get caught.*

My gaze darted between the target building and its neighbor, assessing my options. Three stories up sat my target's office. Not a terrible height, but the walls were maddeningly smooth. Whoever designed this place clearly valued security over aesthetics. The neighboring home loomed a good story higher. I could work with that.

Moving to the back of the property until I found a tree that lifted me halfway up the neighboring home. From there I was back to reaching for each windowsill, burning the muscles of my arms as I hauled myself higher. When I made it to the final windowsill, my hands were raw. The rough brick had shredded my unprotected palms.

Above me, the edge of the roof hung just beyond my reach. Launching upward, I grasped for the hard edge with bleeding fingers. My grip failed.

My feet scrambled for purchase on the now-treacherous windowsill. My right foot slid free, my heart thundering at the thought of falling three stories down.

A fall from this height would shatter bones if I was lucky, kill me if I wasn't. What use was a crippled assassin? Vanya's words echoed in my mind - getting caught or getting dead, same difference.

I slammed my knee against the ledge, pressing myself against filthy windowpanes. The impact surely alerted anyone inside. In desperation, I brought my foot back beneath me, gathered myself and used every bit of strength to leap towards the roof.

Shadows streamed from my fingertips as I reached, and for a heartbeat, I wished they could bridge the gap. Just as despair set in, I felt that too familiar rough surface.

I gripped it tightly and swung myself up, rolling onto the rooftop. For a moment, I just lay there, gasping and listening for any inquiring minds seeking the source of the commotion of my climb. Drawing more shadows around me before I rolled to peer beyond the edge. Not a soul in sight.

Focusing on my mission, I aligned myself to the office window and leapt through the frail glass.

"What in—" A burly voice bellowed from beside me. On the sofa sprawled my target, one woman kneeling before him in a compromising position, the other pressed against his side. The women screamed and fled. Cheap ale, sweat, and cloying perfume fouled the air.

I stalked toward him. His face reddened with every step I took.

"Gold! I'll give you gold, jewels, anything!" He scrambled backward, fighting with his trousers.

Shadows wrapped around me until I vanished. The man glanced around wildly as I moved behind him. Sweat beaded on his brow, his unwashed body reeking of fear.

He whimpered as I grabbed him by his limp blonde hair, my blade pressed against his throat.

"Please, I'll do anything," he begged, his body trembling beneath my grip. My silence terrified him more than words. His marked death would satisfy someone—at least he died true to form: a coward.

I drew my dagger across his neck in one clean stroke. His sobs caught in his throat, body slow to realize its fate. His eyes grew glassy and his chest stilled. Hearing footsteps thundering down the hall—I dove through the shattered window, leaping without another glance.

Rolling as I landed, I sprinted toward Vanya, cloaked in shadows.

Rounding the final corner, I spotted Vanya lounging against a wooden shed. I released my shadows and she gave me a slow clap.

"Not bad," Vanya purred, her feline grin gleaming in the darkness. "We'll work on your subtlety, but you're alive and uncaught. That's a win in my book." She clapped me on the shoulder, guiding me through the labyrinth of shadowy alleys.

The silence suited me. My mind wandered between memorizing our path and grappling with my first contracted kill. Shame gnawed at me—what would my grandmother think? She'd probably beat me with her favorite pan, if she didn't kill me outright for becoming this monster. If she were still alive, I'd be home with her instead of stalking the night for prey.

"What's next?" I asked, my voice barely above a whisper as the weight of my actions settled over me like a shroud.

CHAPTER 16

We approached large, iron gates. Beyond them lay a winding path and in the distance, a dark manor stood. Trees peppered the property near the gates.

"Now, I'll show you to your room and get you some new clothes. I bet Cook has something for us to eat if you're hungry." Vanya took a key from her cloak and shoved it into the metal structure. It groaned as she twisted it and pushed the gates open. Once we were inside, she engaged the lock once more. "Tomorrow you begin the real training, get some sleep, you're going to need it."

The manor's interior defied my expectations. Opulent patterns adorned the main receiving room, with pretty trinkets scattered across the mantle and table tops. A grand staircase could be seen from the doorway. She led me up the burgundy steps, the handrail golden like the many details that littered the town.

"Kitchens, weaponry, and common rooms are downstairs," she explained as we turned down a hall. Beautiful artwork hung from the walls in carved, golden frames. The walls themselves had been stained a dark color, almost matching the wooden flooring. Each door we passed was painted red. Blood red. "Most of the rooms on the second floor are bedrooms for guild members, you can find mine at the far end of the hall. Everyone has their own, even if they choose to live in their apartments in town." She stopped at the fifth door on the right, "This one's yours." She opened the door, moonlight spilled from a large window. The room mirrored the manor's interior, luxurious yet tasteful. A four-poster bed sat against the wall, while a desk and wardrobe were the only other pieces of furniture. All were made from rich oak with bronzed accents. I looked around, finding a door leading to a simple ensuite. Upon returning to the main room, Vanya pulled some clothes from the wardrobe and set them on the bed.

"Go ahead and have yourself a bath. Here's a nightshirt and some basics for tomorrow. With the payment from tonight, we'll go get you fitted with something more useful." She nodded as she strode back towards the doorway. "I'll have Cook bring you up something. Try not to let the others have your head before the morning." She laughed as she sauntered out, closing the door behind her.

I sat on the bed for a moment, its plush violet quilt soft to the touch. I'd never stayed in a room so nice. You could've easily fit two of my old bedrooms within it. As nice as luxury was, it made me miss home. My tiny little village with familiar warm faces. My grandmother's laugh rang through the air as she tended her garden. Maël's fingers entwined in mine. My heart ached, and I twisted the ring on my necklace thinking of him, of the life we could've shared. That life never included this, though, but he would've loved the bed. I pressed down on the mattress, feeling the cloud-like plush, softer than anything we had in our cottages.

I grabbed the nightshirt and retreated into the bathroom to draw a hot bath, finding some scented salts to add to the steaming water. After stripping myself bare, I eased into the water, the steam caressing me like my own shadows. Tomorrow was a new day, in my new life, one step closer to my goal. I let the stress from today release its hold on me. The deed was done, I took the life of a man I didn't know, and I didn't even know what he had done to deserve it. I shook the thought of killing an innocent man from my mind. I could beat myself up over being a murderer in the morning.

After getting out and finding a tray of food on the desk, I found no other signs of the person who had brought it. I took a few nibbles but ultimately resolved to sleep. Climbing under the thick covers, I laid my head on the pillows, looking out towards the window, hoping I hadn't condemned my soul for all eternity.

The moonlight cast long shadows across the room, their dance eerily reminiscent of the shadows I could now control. As I settled into the unfamiliar comfort of the bed, the scent of lavender from my bath mingled with a metallic undertone that clung to my skin, a reminder of the life I'd taken. The silence of the manor was oppressive, broken only by the occasional creak of ancient wood and the whisper of wind through the trees outside. I closed my eyes, but sleep eluded me, my mind a whirlwind of conflicting emotions: guilt, fear, and a treacherous spark of exhilaration at the power I now possessed.

CHAPTER 17

My stomach churned at sunrise. In this strange bed, reality hit me—I'd soon head downstairs to start my new life with assassins. Part of me wanted to flee, but I had nowhere else to go. Despite Vanya's warning, I was alive. Maybe they weren't the monsters I'd feared. I crept from bed to the desk where Vanya's clothes waited. The black leather pants fit, though long, revealing her taller build. The tight black shirt rode up above my waist. I'd have to manage with ill-fitting clothes - one more sign I didn't belong. Yet.

After pulling on my boots and strapping the dagger to my thigh, I tucked my dark hair behind my pointed ears for clear sight. Taking a breath, I stepped out.

Following the noise downstairs, I found the dining room. Voices and laughter filled the space where two laden tables stretched end to end. Men crowded around heaping plates as I searched for an empty seat.

"Hey, fresh meat!" A fair haired man called out, gesturing to the empty seat beside him. At least there was no question about their profession - or their capacity for murder. I slid into the offered seat, reaching for the nearest pitcher. Relief washed over me as water, not alcohol, filled my cup. Though I enjoyed my drinks, staying clear-headed seemed wise in unfamiliar territory.

"So, you're Vanya's latest stray?" He asked through his food, eyes bright with interest. He looked harmless enough - golden-haired with warm brown eyes flecked with amber. But assassins weren't meant to look dangerous. Like me—just a slight girl with oversized violet eyes. That was the whole point.

I shrugged, piling food onto my plate. Barely eating the night before had left me ravenous. My hunger clawed at my insides like a feral beast.

"Most of us, yeah," he replied, washing down his food with a swig from his cup. "Name's Lucas."

"Lor," I managed between bites. The buttery biscuit melted on my tongue, its flaky layers reminding me of Sally, our village baker. No one could match her skill with bread, but these came close.

"Not much for conversation, huh?" Lucas mused. "Don't worry, you're not alone. See Jimmy over there?" He nodded toward a hulking figure at the other table. "Took him two whole months to break his silence."

"I'm shocked he managed to resist your sparkling wit for so long."

Lucas flashes a sheepish grin as he leans by my ear, "Well, he threatened to cut my balls off when I tried the first week. I'm a little attached to them and didn't want to risk being maimed." He chuckles at the memory while my cheeks heat up.

"Noted. I'll keep that threat in my back pocket for when you inevitably annoy me."

"Careful, Lor. I might just enjoy that," he said with a wink. Before us, the empty seats were suddenly claimed by a mountain of a man and two burly thugs. The man's eye was covered by a patch while the other, a muddy brown as lifeless as stagnant water, scrutinized me. His two cronies were leering at me like I was their next meal.

"Back off, Lucas. This one's got standards," the man growled, his single eye boring into Lucas, who visibly tensed.

"I do have standards," I shot back, refusing to let this brute intimidate me. Either I showed my teeth now, or I'd be prey forever. The man began to howl with laughter at my retort, "Don't flatter yourself, Patches. I prefer my men with depth perception."

The hall quieted into a deafening silence as every head turned in our direction. His cronies gaped like landed fish.

"You'd do well to watch that tongue of yours," Patches snarled, his single eye narrowing as his muscles coiled beneath the table. My first day and I'd already made an enemy. I tensed, expecting a blade, but Donovan just stood with his gang. "The name's Donovan. Remember it." He stormed out with his followers. The hall stayed quiet for a moment before whispers broke out—likely about the new girl foolish enough to taunt their one-eyed leader.

"That was quite the performance, Lor," Lucas said, his eyes darkening with worry. He quickly cleared his plate and rose, nodding towards the exit. "Come on, you're with me today."

"I don't need a babysitter, Lucas. I can handle myself."

"Trust me, getting on Donovan's hit list isn't what concerns me. Vanya assigned us as partners for tonight's job. Said something about complementary skills."

I followed Lucas from the hall to the back gardens' training ring. "What happened to your previous partner?" I asked, testing unfamiliar daggers from the weapons rack.

"She died," Lucas said quietly, hefting a pair of swords and testing their balance. "Ever used these before?" He tossed me the lighter blade. I caught it with practiced ease, testing its weight with a few practiced movements before falling into a ready stance, my lips curving into a confident smile.

"Oh, this is going to be interesting," Lucas said, his eyes lighting up as our blades met in a fierce dance.

We sparred until we both dripped sweat, matching each other's skill. Lucas switched between weapons to test me. My guard training showed—I wielded swords with passable skill, moved like liquid grace with daggers, and my arrows found their marks with deadly accuracy, drawing an appreciative whistle from Lucas.

"You're a natural," he said. The praise felt empty—I'd chosen this path from desperation, not desire. But when Lucas grabbed the battle axes, my skill faltered. Their bulk made them impossible to control.

My confidence wavered when Lucas hefted the battle axes from the weapons rack. The weapons proved too unwieldy, their weight hampering both my strikes and defensive maneuvers.

Throughout the match, shadows beckoned at the edges of my awareness, tempting me to slip into their embrace. I could have danced through the shadows, emerging wherever Lucas left himself vulnerable. Vanya's motives for pairing us remained unclear—had she told him about my... abilities?

Despite my initial reservations, Lucas was growing on me. His endless chatter and easy smiles masked a lethal precision that emerged with each weapon he wielded.

Like watching winter frost claim autumn leaves, his transformation from jovial companion to hardened killer was mesmerizing.

"That's enough for today," he said, his killer's mask melting back into an easy smile. "Get some food and rest. We move at nightfall—be ready."

I nodded, helping Lucas rack the weapons before heading back. Near the manor, I spotted Donovan in the shadows, his single eye gleaming with hate as he watched me, arms crossed over his chest. Though a chill ran down my spine, I kept my head high until he disappeared from sight. I was beginning to regret my clever quip about his depth perception.

CHAPTER 18

As the last rays of sunlight faded, I slipped into my black leathers Vanya had left for me during my training. Upon returning to my room, I discovered several sets of the same items, a few tunic options, and some extra daggers and arrows.

I braided my hair tightly on the sides of my head to keep it out of my face. I lined my eyes with the kohl left on the vanity. The dark substance made my violet eyes pop. It seemed unnecessary, but it was for me. Looking at myself, I felt fierce. For the first time, I didn't see Alora the village huntress, Alora who followed Maël around like a lovesick puppy. I was...more. I was vengeance, I was power, and with newfound confidence, I was beautiful. This transformation felt like shedding an old skin, revealing a deadlier, more confident version of myself. For once, I wasn't defined by my past, I was forging a new identity with every breath.

A knock came from the door, and I grabbed a black cloak, securing my bow and arrows over it and placing my daggers in every sheath on my bodice, along my thighs, and in my boots. Lucas arrived as promised, just as darkness fully settled. Looking me up and down, he let out a low whistle.

"Did you dress up just for me, sweetness?"

"You wish," I rolled my eyes and pushed past him through the doorway.

"You have no idea, but we have a job to do and we can discuss fun later." He winked. We made our way out of the manor and traveled down the dirt road leading to the gates leading to town. Lucas told me we're doing some recon on a meeting, we're not supposed to engage yet unless necessary. The client wanted intel on their target's meeting and motives. Simple enough—I could ditch Lucas briefly and use my power to find a good spot to observe.

He led us towards an old barn, worn with age, the main doors sagged into each other. We dropped into the bushes a short distance before, making our final strategy.

"Can you climb?" he asked as he watched the building.

I nodded, and he smiled.

"Good, get up on the rafters and listen from up there, I'm going to sneak in from the back and try to get close enough. Remember, don't engage unless necessary. Meet me back here once they leave and try not to get yourself killed."

With that, we split up, and once he disappeared around the bend, I willed shadows to wrap around me, blending me into the natural shadows of the building. Walking around the opposite side of the large barn, I found a couple of barrels stacked by the loft opening. I climbed atop them, wary of their ability to hold even my weight, before leaping up towards the opening. My fingertips barely grasped the ledge as I swung my legs over to gain purchase into the loft. Thankfully, no one was already hiding up here as I checked my surroundings. Not that they would see a person, but I'm sure a moving shadow would create some havoc.

I took light steps as I tiptoed towards the end of the platform, looking out over the rest of the barn. I didn't see Lucas on the far side ahead of me, so either he's hidden really well or he's hidden somewhere below the loft. I crouched on the railing near the ladder, a dagger already poised in my hand just in case.

Two cloaked men entered, speaking quietly. They discussed a trade while unaware of us watching. Though they spoke in code, it became clear this was about human trafficking, not drugs. They set the next exchange for the docks in a few days. I wanted to shoot them both, but our mission was intel - the client needed to find where the victims were held. Killing these men now would only delay the next exchange and leave the captives unfound.

Once they left, I waited a few beats before banishing my shadows. Moving out of the loft to head to our meetup bush, Lucas wasn't there yet, so I crouched and kept an eye out towards the road. A twig snapped behind me, and I turned, thinking it's him, but before I could lay eyes on Lucas, I'm struck from behind. My vision faded to black, the world spinning into a kaleidoscope of shadows. The last thing I registered was the cold bite of metal against my skin and the acrid taste of fear rising in my throat.

WAKE UP, Lor. You need to get up right now. Please, gods, wake up.

I woke bound to a chair in a musty barn. The ropes at my wrists were tight, unyielding. Lucas sat tied across from me, groaning. My stomach dropped as reality set in. Those two men had somehow overpowered us, dragging us here. Past Lucas, the barn door slid open and Donovan entered with his men, smirking like they'd won a prize.

"Well, well, look who's finally awake," Donovan sneered, his face inches from mine. "Ready to introduce yourself properly to Jasper and Erick? It'd be a shame to kill you before they had the pleasure."

"Back off, Donovan," Lucas snarled, straining against his bonds.

"Can't handle a little teasing from the new girl? Your ego that fragile?" One of Donovan's goons—Jasper or Erick, I couldn't tell which—silenced him with a vicious gut punch.

Donovan's eyes gleamed with malice as he circled Lucas. "You've been a thorn in my side for too long. I won't make the mistake of letting you live again." He leaned in close, his voice dropping to a cruel whisper. "I wonder, will you beg as sweetly as your sister did?" His blade flashed in the dim light, pressing against Lucas's exposed throat. "She was so eager to trade her life for yours. What a waste."

"Stop!" I screamed. "Your issue's with me, Patches." I knew provoking him was stupid, but I couldn't watch Lucas die for my mistake. Donovan spun toward me like a predator spotting prey. Two strides and he was there, his blade slicing my thigh, blood soaking my pants.

"Eager to die first?" Donovan's voice dripped with venom as he traced the dagger along my jawline, the cold steel a whisper away from drawing blood. "Will you beg for mercy? Plead for forgiveness?" His hot breath hissed in my ear, "Or maybe you'll service me before I cut your throat?" Bile rose as I realized—he meant to kill us both. I needed time, had to give Lucas a chance. I glimpsed him working his bonds while Jasper and Erick beat him, his face bruised and swollen.

"Eyes on me," Donovan growled, his face inches from mine. "I want to savor the moment you realize death has come for you." The world exploded in pain as his fist connected with my face. My nose went numb instantly. He rained blows and slashes upon me until I was nothing but a bloody, battered mess slumped in the chair. Through the haze of agony, I focused on working my wrists against the rope. If I could just free one hand, I might have a chance to distract him.

"Trying to escape, are we?" Donovan's voice was a feral growl as he hefted me, chair and all, and hurled me into one of the stable doors. Pain erupted through my body as wood splintered beneath me. Before I could even attempt to move, he was on me, his weight crushing the air from my lungs. His blade bit into my wrists, opening rivers of crimson. Fists rained down on my face and abdomen as he snarled, "Tell me, little mouse. Does death terrify you?"

To fear death the way Donovan sought in my eyes, one needed something worth living for. He searched for that desperate glimmer, that wordless plea to cling to life. But for me, death had long been a familiar shadow, a potential reunion with Grandmother and Maël. I'd spent countless nights wondering about the afterlife, imagining my village existing beyond the veil, untouched by tragedy. Part of me hoped Maël had been with me all along, but that would deny him his eternal peace. Whatever awaited me in death, I would face it unflinching. But it would not come at the hands of this brutish, one-eyed thug.

"No," I spat, a mouthful of blood splattering across Donovan's face. My lips curled into a crimson smile as I locked eyes with him. "To fear death, I'd need something to live for. Death and I are old friends. I'll embrace him gladly when he comes." With the last reserves of my strength, I called upon the darkness. It rushed in, a tide of impenetrable black that swallowed everything. In that moment of blindness, my dagger found Donovan's throat, its starlight blade a ghostly shimmer in the void. A wet gurgle, then the sudden absence of his weight told me he'd fallen, his life pooling beneath him. I summoned shadows to wrap my bleeding wrists and legs, a feeble attempt to stem the flow. When I reached Lucas, Jasper and Erick were gone, likely fled in the chaos of Donovan's demise. I sliced through Lucas's bonds and dispelled the darkness. He was battered and bruised, but alive.

"What in the hells was that?" Lucas's eyes widened as they fell on Donovan's lifeless form. "Did you—" His words trailed off as his head lolled back.

"We need to leave. Now." I hauled Lucas to his feet, wrapping my arm around his waist and bracing him against my shoulder. Together, we stumbled out of the blood-soaked barn.

CHAPTER 19

The journey back dragged on endlessly, with us barely able to take a full stride between the two of us. I silently prayed we'd make it back. Lucas didn't deserve to suffer for my reckless mouth.

The rhythmic thudding of horse hooves sounded behind me. I closed my eyes, begging for it to be someone who would go right past us, not noticing our bleak state. My silent prayers weren't answered as they slowed beside us, and I peered over to find a silver-haired man on the bench of the wagon.

"Aye, you look like you could use a ride." The man didn't gawk at our bloody state. "Climb in, I can take ye up the road."

I shook my head. "That's okay, we're fine."

"Lass, you're bloody well not fine. I won't ask again, and I won't ask about what happened. Just don't get any ideas about robbing me."

I sighed. It was clear he wasn't going to leave us alone if we continued as we were. I helped Lucas up onto the bench and sat beside him, my hand poised on my leg, ready to draw a weapon.

"What brings you out so late, you know the roads are dangerous. I've heard there's bandits out here." I tried to keep my voice calm.

"I don't think bandits are interested in books, girl. Plus, I've been traveling this way to visit my sister for years now. Never have I come across anyone unsavory."

He eyed Lucas, who was now passed out on my shoulder. "Is your friend alive?"

"Yeah, just got into a fight he couldn't win."

The old man chuckled. "I know what that's like."

"So you're a book merchant?" I asked, my fingers itching to browse his collection. Books were my weakness, and even in this dire situation, I couldn't help my curiosity.

"Aye, are you needing anything?" We reached the top of the road where the two diverging paths took you to town or the manor respectively. He pulled the carriage to a stop and helped me wake Lucas up enough for him to stand.

I passed him my pouch of coin. "I'll take whatever this will get me."

He weighed the pouch in his hands before digging through his wares, pulling out a blue leather volume. "Keep your coin, consider it a gift. Try not to let your friend start any more fights." He handed me the book and my coin pouch back, and I tucked them in my bag before grabbing hold of Lucas. I called out a thanks as the old man took off into the night.

"I'm so sorry, Lor," Lucas mumbled.

"I'm sorry, Lucas." I huffed as I kept just moving towards the gates. We were almost there. "I guess we're friends now, huh?"

He let out a painful laugh. "You're not getting rid of me that easily."

I laughed as I dragged us through the property and through the doors. The weight of Lucas against my side had become familiar in our trek, like carrying a wounded brother. I wasn't sure which room was his, so I brought him to mine to mend him. The soft glow of candlelight cast dancing shadows across his battered face as I settled him at my desk, thankful he was more awake than he had been. My hands trembled slightly as I grabbed bandages, ointment, and a rag from my drawers, the reality of the night's events finally catching up to me. With gentle movements born of practice I didn't know I had, I began cleaning his wounds.

The battered man winced as I slathered the ointment on his open cuts. My hands shook slightly as I worked, guilt gnawing at my chest with each pained breath he took. "Is it too late to discuss the fun part of the evening?" A hoarse chuckle from his chest betrayed he's trying not to appear as hurt as he is. Purple bruises bloomed across his ribs where I dabbed the cloth, and he flinched each time I found another hidden cut beneath his torn shirt.

"What do you mean? This is the fun part," I replied dryly, though my heart ached knowing I'd brought this violence upon him. Finally finishing wrapping his wounds, I helped him onto the bed.

"Now this is what I'm talking about," he murmured as he let out a heavy sigh as he drifted off to sleep, his body succumbing to exhaustion. The pain etched across his face slowly melted away, replaced by the peaceful expression of deep slumber.

I perched on the edge of the desk, watching the steady rise and fall of his chest. Strange how quickly someone could go from stranger to friend, how fierce the need to protect them could become. Lucas had stood by me tonight when he didn't have to, and I silently vowed to never let him face such danger alone again.

CHAPTER 20

Two years had passed since that fateful night Donovan crossed me at the farm. In the time since, Lucas and I had become an inseparable team. We weren't flawless, but we got the job done more often than not. He's a skilled thief, a trait he attributes to having to scrounge on the streets with his sister. Every day, I learned something new about him. He's still overly friendly to new members, and as it did with me, it always freaks them out. One recruit was so unnerved, he brandished a butter knife at Lucas in defense.

This morning we sat in Vanya's opulent office, the air thick with anticipation. Lucas propped his foot on her oak desk, an elbow resting on the wooden arm of the dark upholstered chair, twirling a knife in his hand. I rolled my eyes at the childish grin he flashed me.

The thick door separating the office from the hallway creaked open and I heard the light even footfalls of our master. She paused behind Lucas, plucking the knife from his hand like a snake striking. Her fingers pressed against the blade end, no fear of the potential risk of cutting herself.

"If your foot ever graces my desk again, Lucas, you'll find yourself answering to 'Peggy,'" she threatened, her voice a lethal whisper as she glided to her high-backed chair. Lucas, not one to ignore an obvious hint, removed his foot, adjusting himself in his seat with a grunt. Vanya stared him down, almost as if she could threaten his very soul one more time before continuing.

"Tonight, you'll attend the Governor's ball," she said, her gaze shifting between us. "Your target wears a purple jacket with a blue feather. He's meeting an associate." Her eyes locked on mine. "Gather the intel, but do not engage. Remain undetected at all costs. Is that clear?"

"Understood," we chorused, our voices blending in perfect unison.

"Good," Vanya nodded, satisfaction glinting in her eyes. "Lor, you'll gather the intel. Lucas, keep watch. If anything seems off, you both leave immediately. Some attendees... well, let's just say I'd prefer they didn't notice you."

She reached into her desk drawer, producing two masks. "Your attire will be sent up shortly. You'll need these." The masks clattered onto the desk, half-face designs, Lucas' in black silk, mine in delicate black lace.

A wicked smile curved Vanya's lips. "I trust you both can dance?" She waved us off with a chuckle. "Your carriage arrives in an hour. Don't be late."

MY HANDS GLIDED over the gown that had been waiting for me upon my return to my room. The neckline descended in a deep V, nearly reaching my navel. Black silk clung to my body, with delicate lace tracing every edge. The corset top and long skirt, while revealing, provided me enough structure to stash six of my obsidian throwing knives, my favorite dagger strapped high on my thigh.

Gods, I wish I was escorting you tonight, Maël's voice growled in my mind. *You look absolutely ravishing.*

I let out a soft sigh as I examined myself in the mirror. Gone was the village girl who once stumbled home caked in training yard dirt. Tonight I appeared elegant, even I had to acknowledge my body has filled out in a way I never thought it would, a testament to no longer scrounging for meals. The daily training had sculpted my muscles, making my limbs leaner and more toned. I gathered part of my hair up, leaving the remainder to cascade below my shoulders. I rimmed my eyes with kohl before slipping on the dainty slippers that match my ensemble. I winced at the flimsy feeling soles, wishing my boots could be worn instead. I brushed a rosy pink color on my lips and with a final check, I glided out the door to meet Lucas in the courtyard.

He stood in a dark suit beside the carriage, and though I couldn't see anything, I knew he'd concealed several weapons beneath his formal attire. His gaze traced the length of my body as I drew near, and he whistled low and flashed me a sly smile as he moved towards me, placing a hand at the small of my back to guide me to our transportation for the night.

"Getting you to that meeting unseen may be more difficult than we anticipated," he whispered into my ear as he opened the carriage door, helping me inside. He joined me in and settled beside me on the bench. With a tap on the outside of the window, we're off towards the Governor's large home. "You look lovely, Lor."

"I'll manage just fine," I gave him a wide grin before wreathing myself in shadows, giving him a glimpse of why they called me Death's Wraith.

"Well, look at you without the training yard grime. Almost didn't recognize you," I teased.

He chuckled as I dispersed my shadows. We refined our strategy as we journeyed along the winding roads. Upon arrival, we'll mingle, blend in with the attendees until our mark shows. Though I'd never learned these court dances, Lucas promised to guide me through them. Once I see the target head to the meeting, I'll find a spot to conceal myself and follow him. We settled on a meetup outside the gates.

The carriage rolled along until we drew up beside large wrought iron gates standing open in welcome to the sprawling white mansion beyond them. As we came to a stop, our driver leapt off his perch to open the door. Lucas stepped out first, spinning to hold his hand out to me. I gently placed my hand in his as I emerged, trying to emulate the other graceful nobles in attendance.

The carriage pulled away as we approached the large doors. Attendants in frilly green uniforms stood on either side welcoming guests as they filed in. Once we passed the threshold, we joined those before us in a grand ballroom. It seemed like a million candles illuminated the room, making it as bright as the sun this kingdom's monarch was known to worship. Men and women waltzed around the dance floor in gowns and suits of every color. Tables laden with food bordered the walls. Guards in gilded uniforms stood throughout the room. A quick assessment told me it would be unwise to draw attention to ourselves.

Lucas leads us to the couples gracefully gliding, twirling me to face him, his hand keeping hold of my own, his other securing itself to my waist. I rest my other on his shoulder as he takes measured steps, following the direction of the crowd. I'm trying not to trip or step on him while the music seems to urge us faster and faster. While we appear to be looking at each other, as lovers would, we're both searching for our target. Every twirl of the dance gives us the perfect opportunity to pivot and assess a new area of the ballroom. Soon, the song shifts to something more calm, steady, unlike the quick tempo we had been following before.

Lucas leaned close, his lips near my ear, "You won't like this next part, but you're dancing beautifully. We're almost done. When the music changes, we'll switch partners. We'll step away and come together, palm to palm, then turn and I must move on to the woman beside us and another man will meet you palm to palm. Just follow his lead like you've been doing. The steps should be simple like this for a bit."

I barely had time to meet his eyes, fearing being left to my own devices in this situation. As promised, we joined the line of couples, stepped apart, then pressed our palms together. Lucas gave me a wink, his reassuring smile not quite reaching the edges of his mask, before turning to sweep the brunette beside us into his arms. She brightened at his touch, her hand trailing coyly across his chest as they danced away.

A warm palm met mine as deep brown eyes captured my gaze. A midnight blue mask adorned the face before me, the male so tall I had to tilt my head back to meet his stare. Dark waves of hair nearly concealed the pointed fae ears beneath. His suit matched his mask, fine silver stitching catching the light. As he drew me closer, the subtle scent of rain and leather enveloped me, reminiscent of rainy days spent dodging Lucas's attacks. The familiar scent helped steady my nerves, bringing my focus back to the task at hand.

The stranger remained silent, moving through the steps as mechanically as I did. I followed his lead, grateful for the even tempo. As we glided across the floor, I spotted a violet suit near a table laden with cakes. I fixed my gaze on its wearer—a man with closely cropped blonde hair, shorter than me, sporting a bulbous nose and a delicate blue feather in his pocket. He pulled out a golden watch, scanned the room, then slipped past nearby guests down a hallway to my left.

The dance brought another turn. Once facing the stranger again, I released his hand and dropped into a curtsy.

"Thank you for a lovely dance," I said before turning away.

"W-wait!" He called after me. Heavy footsteps followed, and I cursed myself knowing he pursued me. I pretended not to hear, weaving through the crowd in search of Lucas or an escape. After several turns through dense clusters of people, I risked a glance behind. The tall stranger stood searching the crowd, and guilt pricked at me. His head snapped toward me, and he hurried to close the distance. I rushed toward the dark hallway, discreetly sliding knives from my corset as I reached the archway. If I couldn't shake him, I'd need to resort to desperate measures. Vanya would have my head.

The hallway's darkness was a welcome relief after the bright ballroom. Before I could summon my shadows, a drunk couple crashed into me. I caught myself against the cold stone wall, my knife clattering to the floor. Their collision pushed me into an alcove - both a blessing and a curse. I glimpsed my pursuer through my stumble, but the alcove's cover let me pull shadows around myself until I was nearly invisible. Steadying myself, I peered around the corner. The stranger stood in the archway surveying the hall, disappointment clear on his masked face. I hurried deeper into the passage until it curved, spotting the man in the purple suit checking his watch once more before slipping through a door ahead.

By the time I reached it, the door was shut, and voices within warned against reopening it. Crouching by the metal knob, I listened carefully.

"...Tyrian will ensure the package is delivered at the docks in three days time..."

A few moments of eavesdropping confirmed we had what we needed. I had the name, location, and date for Vanya—mission accomplished. The lively party still called to me, but I kept my shadows close until I found Lucas beyond the gates. We returned to the manor and delivered the intelligence to Vanya, who promised to inform one of us when she was ready to move. While I retreated to my quarters to shed my frilly attire, Lucas sauntered off in search of tavern mischief.

CHAPTER 21

The next morning, Lucas practically skipped to our usual table in the dining room. He wasted no time piling his plate high, a Cheshire grin spreading across his face.

"I believe I know something you don't," he teased in between bites.

I peered at him over my mug of coffee, internally sighing with dismay. "I am perfectly fine with not knowing the details about your conquests from the night prior." Lucas loved to find lonely travelers at the local tavern and keep them company. Never for more than one night, always keeping his distance.

He feigned offense, "His name was Ralph and I swear it was over 10 inches!" I shook my head at him while he let out a melodious laugh. "A little birdie told me there's some fun to be had tonight. You in?"

Vanya must be ready to send us out after the intel we gathered. Lucas was grinning like a crazed child about to devour a barrel full of sweets. "Only if you promise to keep your tales about Ralph to yourself."

"I'll make no such promises, how else am I to prevent you from becoming a shrew?"

"Some people are better off alone, Lucas," I rose from my seat. "See you at the gates later?"

He nodded, continuing with his meal as I sauntered out the dining hall doors. It was time to sharpen my blades.

TWILIGHT HAD SETTLED over the manor when I met Lucas at the gates. He leaned casually against a post, dressed in dark leathers, impatiently flicking one of his knives.

"Took ya long enough," he shoved his blade back in its sheath. "Did you have enough time to primp my lady?"

I swung my hips as I strode past him, pushing my braid behind my shoulder and looking back at him, fluttering my eyelashes. "Why yes, kind sir, I had just enough time to sharpen every blade strapped to me."

"I bow before your deadly grace, my queen."

He swept into an exaggerated bow, flourishing his arm with theatrical grace. "Shall we paint the town red, my lady?"

Our shared mockery dissolved into genuine laughter as we headed toward town, our laughter echoing in the night air.

There was a time when laughter felt like a forgotten language. But Lucas had taught me to speak it again, even if I remained broken inside. Like scattered pieces of a mirror, he helped me find the fragments that still caught the light. It wasn't much, but it was enough to keep breathing, to keep moving forward.

Each mission also provided the perfect distraction while I kept my eyes and ears out for Johan. This time would be no different. The intel I gathered had us paying a visit to a human trafficker named

Tyrian. Vanya deemed it was time to pay him a visit before he could deliver his wares to his clients. While we would be busy wrangling him, she had separate teams dealing with the clients and the poor souls who ever crossed paths with Tyrian and his men. By the end of the night, each victim would get sent to a sanctuary or returned to their previous lives. It was the best we could do.

We discussed our plan, our voices low and urgent. Tyrian lived near the square. We'd approach from an alley, where I'd cloak us in shadows. Then, we'd slip in through a window. I'd take the front, Lucas the upper level.

The mission was simple enough, a quiet execution. At least, that's what I was hoping for.

The moon hung high as we slipped into the neighborhood, melting into the alley shadows. Late-night merchants hawked snacks and potions, their hushed voices barely masking sly deals. Despite the hour, the cobblestone streets bustled with life, drunk men and giggling women stumbling past, oblivious to the two assassins lurking in the darkness.

We surveyed the home of our target. An imposing but quaint brick townhome set between four other houses. We'd have to cross the road in order to access the property. The windows along the sides seemed like our best point of entry since trees sat as sentries along the front fence and curved towards the building.

I nodded towards the house and knocked Lucas on the shoulder, "Let's go." I pulled the shadows of the alley towards us, cloaking us in a dark haze. We've done this bit so many times, I didn't even have to chide my partner on following closely behind. Any step out of place would leave him exposed.

I guided us through the darkest areas of the road until we reached the other side, just a house away from where we needed to be. Taking slow steps, we were able to avoid the merchants and people enjoying the balmy night. From the neighboring yard, we pushed through the line of trees and reached the lower window.

With a quick look to ensure no one was looking in our direction, Lucas used his dagger to pry the window open. The sound of the lock breaking was quiet, eerily so. I reminded myself for what felt like the hundredth time not to piss him off. As childish and kind as he can be, beyond that cute face was a man ready to take and kill anything that crossed his path.

We crawled through the window and took stock of area. A long table with a white marbled top took up most of the space with ten carved, white chairs surrounding it. While it's dark in here, the room just beyond the foyer emitted a warm glow and an obnoxious sound ringing throughout the floor. I disbanded my shadows around us. I followed my friend as we crept towards the room. We came to a receiving room, the fireplace lit with Tyrian passed out in a patchy blue armchair facing the flames. The ornate rug below our feet made it easy to cover each step as we snuck behind the unassuming man, Lucas gravitating towards the other side so we could nab him without issue. As I got close enough to start making out his features, his eyes opened wide and I felt the breeze as something whipped out in front of me. Tyrian jumped up onto the cushioned seat, brandishing his weapon...a fucking fire poker.

"I don't remember inviting guests over tonight." His eyes narrowed, flitting between Lucas and I as we pulled daggers into our hands.

"Aw, don't hurt my feelings Tyrian," Lucas cooed, his feet inching him closer, "let's put down the poker and have a nice conversation, yeah?"

"A *nice* conversation?!" Tyrian spat, he swiped the poker towards Lucas, causing the man to take a step back to avoid its sharp point. The criminal spun and launched the poker at me as he jumped from his perch. As I pivoted to avoid the flying object, I tried to grab the man before he could escape. He jumped farther than I thought and I barely caught his legs, sending us both crashing to the floor. Lucas tackled him, resulting in the three of us wrestling on the hard floor.

Look up Lor!

I saw the flash of steel before the familiar sound of a blade slashing by. We're lucky he's got poor aim with the weapon, but the distraction of avoiding a slice to the throat gave him the chance to kick us both off. He barreled out his front door, the two of us following in pursuit. I pulled inky tendrils towards us, hiding our identities as much as I could while in pursuit.

Cries rang out in shock as the beaten man ran down the street. I slipped a dagger out and started throwing them towards his legs to try to stop him. As I readied a second after the first narrowly missed, my eyes caught on a large figure chatting with a merchant over a turkey leg. Captain Johan's big ugly face watched as Tyrian hauled himself down the road and I gave chase. I stopped my pursuit for a moment, pointing my blade towards him instead.

I'm knocked in the shoulder. "What the hell do you think you're doing, he's getting away!" Lucas hissed low, glaring at me like I've simultaneously kicked his dog and lost my mind. I shook my head and turned back to the spot Johan stood, the spot now empty.

Lucas pulled me along as we sped past guards in shiny armor shouting and trying to nab us. Tyrian took a turn down an alley and we followed him. Without the risk of hitting someone else and the straight path, I'm able to launch another dagger at the man. The blade sank deep into the back of his neck.

"Hope you're ready for Vanya's wrath. I'll see you at the usual spot!"

With that, Lucas disappeared down the alley, my shadows melting away as he vanished into the darkness.

I sighed, it wasn't like I meant for him to leave his house, but I finally set eyes on the man I've hunted for years. That familiar feeling of bloodlust towards the man who killed my family returning like an old friend. I'll take whatever lashing Vanya saw fit to bestow upon me, I was closer than I've ever been to finishing my revenge.

Or you could let it go. Find a beautiful ocean view, and spend your days reading on the beach.

I felt that familiar hum of adrenaline as voices carried closer to me, not wanting to spend the night in the gallows, I left the alley. Lucas was long gone by the time I emerged from the opening, but that didn't stop me from colliding with a solid body, covered in dark armor. It grunted at the impact, but I didn't stay long enough for it to realize a person had run into them. The hum seemed to turn to a vibration until I put several blocks between me and Tyrian's grave. Leaving me feeling empty and morose over letting Johan escape. Next time, he wouldn't be so fortunate.

CHAPTER 22

I stood before the tavern where I first encountered Vanya. The once rugged bar now felt familiar, like a fragment of home.

Home, I mused, a word I never imagined using again. Yet, I felt tendrils of my new life taking root, much like my village once had.

Every day, I returned to my room in the guild and dined with my fellow outcasts, talking about anything from the weather to telling tales. It was a small feeling of home. I learned the names of the main merchants here in town, knew the best baker (who was NOT the man with the stall in the square), knew this seedy looking bar had the best ale in town. Another small piece of the feeling of being at home being formed. I never thought I'd feel this way again. Each morning, I woke to the hollow ache of my lost village, and each night, I fell asleep with that same emptiness.

Home was a small cottage, hunting in the woods, my grandmother, and my best friend. Home had been razed, turned to ash by my own hand. I shuddered at the thought as I pushed the heavy door open.

Home is whatever and wherever you want it to be... My mind's Maël whispered.

The tavern roared with life, soldiers crowding the tables and women flirting brazenly on their arms. I found a spot in the corner, perfect for me to drown my sorrows without participating in the rowdiness. I failed myself tonight, lost sight of my last connection to that night. Lost the man who enjoyed destroying all that I held dear. I was so close, and yet, I couldn't achieve everything I've been working towards. The long days I've spent learning how to manipulate shadows, hunting not only for survival but in effort to continue weapons training, it felt like it was all for nothing tonight as I watched that horrid man get away.

The barmaid, Evangeline, sauntered up, her face red from the never ending work but no lack of joy could be seen, "What'll you have doll?"

"Just an ale and some bread if you have it," I answered. She nodded as she headed towards the bar, receiving several requests for more ale.

Jones, the barkeep as I've come to find out, must be in a mood tonight. He rushes around the bar, barking orders to the staff, filling tankards of ale and bringing more kegs to the front as he empties them. The men in here must be celebrating to be this excited.

Evangeline is back in no time with a tankard and a piece of bread. I thank her and hand her my coin. I tune out the reveille to drown my sorrows with my own drink. "You're looking a little worse for wear tonight Lor," she chided. "Did a bunny give you the slip?"

Of course, she wasn't referring to an actual bunny. Since joining the guild, I'd maintained a facade of taking odd hunting jobs, primarily for the elderly who couldn't manage themselves. Everyone had some sort of cover story to look a bit legit. Some of the other assassins even owned businesses that "employed" fellow guild members. Vanya's guild wasn't large, but they took care of each other, as if they were a family. Since the tavern was a preferred meeting spot for clients, Jones and Evangeline were aware of Vanya's true occupation and knew most of the guild members. Building this sort of relationship guaranteed Jones a lot of coin from the guild, both for business use and when we would come to drink, his silence was a small price to pay.

I chuckled halfheartedly at Evangeline's remark. "Something like that. I caught the bunny but spotted a tasty deer ahead and thought I could snag both." I took a swig of ale. "But it got away from me."

Evangeline shook her head. "Well, there's always next time for you lot. We've heard how skilled you are, I'm sure it's a matter of time before that deer comes back." She gave me an encouraging smile before scurrying off to help the other patrons. Evangeline always had a kind soul, one I didn't think would be particularly friendly with assassins, but one night she and I had gone far down the bottle and it slipped she had a past she barely scraped away from. Jones was an asshole no doubt, but he didn't beat his employees. Vanya had a rule about only taking jobs against those who were truly wicked, and even a kind soul could look past the murder aspect to see the potential good in it. I admired that about her. Sometimes, I wasn't so sure there was anything good left in myself after a particularly gruesome night.

She's right you know. Maël chided. *Or you can let this whole revenge thing go and live your life.*

I can't let you go, I all but pleaded to my imaginary lover. This is all I have now.

A faint chuckle rang in my head. *You have so much more than you realize, Lor. Open your eyes and your heart and you'll see.*

Already halfway done with my drink and starting to feel the disappointment from tonight slipping away. Open my eyes and heart, yeah right. Despite being a figment of my imagination, the Maël in my head didn't understand me. I surveyed the debauchery and dancing around me, my gaze landing on a pair of light eyes. Instantly, my face reddened even though he was the one staring.

His golden hair was pulled back into a bun, a wide grin stretching across his face as he stood. Handsome didn't begin to describe him, I was beginning to understand why so many called the fae beautiful. His beauty was beyond anything I've seen before, fae or human. I couldn't help but feel I'd betrayed my own heart for these thoughts. I had only ever been attracted to Maël, none of the other men in the village ever came close to catching my eye the way he did. Truthfully, I had resigned to live out my life forever on my own. It was better than marrying anyone else, my heart still belonged to my childhood friend. The man before me almost reminded me of Maël. Confidence and warmth rolled off him in waves, unashamed at being caught in his stare.

His fighting leathers stood in sharp contrast to the gleaming suits of armor that filled the tavern.

My heart thundered against my ribs as his purposeful strides brought him directly to my corner.

Traitor, I chided my racing heart, even as Maël's earlier words about opening my heart echoed mockingly in my mind.

CHAPTER 23

Of course, it's just my luck that he suddenly appears beside me. I brought my ale to my lips, feigning taking a very long, slow sip. I tried not to think about how devastatingly handsome he was up close. The only man I've ever loved was gone and here I was ogling some stranger in a bar. I fought with myself not to continue staring and instead directed my eyes ahead, surveying the rowdy crowd.

His quick glance shifted to a couple dancing—a guard fresh off duty, based on his uniform, with a redheaded woman in blue. Her rouged cheeks and up swept hair complemented her knowing smile as they twirled, lost in each other. He was too drunk to notice anything but her, while she likely eyed his coin purse for later.

"If he continues to spin her around like that they won't be able to walk straight for days," he said to me, nodding towards the couple dancing.

I all but snorted into my cup, watching them spin endlessly on the floor until I met his gaze. It's unwavering this close, amusement sparkling in his eyes.

"It's refreshing to see love in an old tavern." But I knew better.

With this crowd, it was just business—the guard would lose his coin, and if the woman played it right, she'd be counting it later. That's how things worked here.

He laughed and brought his full focus on me. "And here I thought you were too busy looking at me from across the room."

I rolled my eyes at him. "I believe you were the one staring at me. I only just noticed."

He shot me a look that was clear he wasn't ashamed to be caught, "The most beautiful woman in the kingdom just walked through this tavern. I was excited she was blessing me with her attention."

I looked up at him, surely he's joking, not even Maël was so bold. I schooled my face, feigning indifference to his pretty words. "I think you must have mistaken me for one of the other ladies in attendance tonight. Surely you'd prefer someone more prim and proper and not half drunk off one tankard." I nodded towards a stunning blonde with waist-length curls smiling brightly as if one of the men around her said something funny. Her breasts pushed beyond gravity with her tight corset while her waist looked about as thick as my leg. "Perhaps her, she certainly appears to be sun blessed."

He followed my gaze for a moment before returning back to me. "Didn't even notice her, and I'm not sure if sun blessed is the term I would use." He took a sip of his ale, "I'm more interested in the woman who looks ready to fight someone." The statement came out so serious that it caused us both to laugh. His laugh was infectious and suddenly my new favorite sound. I could feel a buzz throughout my body, likely the ale. In all my visits here, I'd only spoken to staff, with others keeping their distance. Unsettling. My days were filled with training, reading, and scouting, while nights I became death's shadow. Ready to fight at any moment, I longed to work out my tonight's failure in the training ring.

Always looking to kick someone's ass. Maël's laugh rang throughout my mind.

"Only someone looking for a fight would be enamored with someone they think would be an opponent," I said, "I'm not interested in screwing up your pretty face tonight, but I'm sure Horace over there would oblige." I gestured to a burly fellow at one of the farther tables. Horace was always ready for a fight, and relished in it, but he was a monster of a brute. You did not want to be on the receiving end of his fists.

I needed to leave, I've spoken too much to this man, spent too long here. It was time to report back and make a plan to find my target. "Good luck and be sure to duck quickly." I nodded as I stood to leave. Maybe this man wouldn't be Horace's next victim.

He stood quickly, stopping me from being able to step away. "What's your name?"

I hesitated. I'd said too much already. Friends and relationships weren't part of my plan—everyone close to me ended up dead. No need to add to that list. But how close could you get to someone you just met? I had to admit, he was charming.

"You can call me Lor."

I met his eyes as he smiled as if he was given the world, "Ryn. It's a pleasure to meet you Lor."

CHAPTER 24

Ryn's presence radiated warmth, like the golden heroes from the pages of my favorite novels.

Ryn was a captain from what he told me, traveling around Sunneva, wherever their orders sent them. I didn't pry much about his work, it was pretty clear from how he skated around the subject and provided vague answers that details weren't on the table. He was a simple man, traveling the kingdom, sleeping under the stars (a particular favorite of his), and in his words "dazzling the world with his amazingness". I couldn't help but giggle as he gave me a sly grin.

"Do you not find me amazing? Did you see this smile?" He pointed to his wide grin.

He forced his smile wider, looking almost manic, making me laugh even harder.

"I didn't quite say that, though your head seems twice as large since I first laid eyes on you." I mused.

"I'll have you know, I have a perfectly proportionally sized head, Love. Mother tells me every time she sees me."

"Oh well, if your mother says so." I took a sip of the ale I've been nursing for the last hour. I could still feel a buzz, I just wasn't sure if it was from my drink or my company.

He finished his drink and surveyed the tavern. Most patrons had left or gone upstairs. Jones cleaned his counter while glaring at Crazy Tom, who ranted about the war, Esmeray, and royal conspiracies. Tom embraced his nickname, even using it when sober—if he ever truly was.

Ryn rested his elbow on the table and propped up his head on his hand, pieces of his blonde hair falling out of the bun atop his head. "You don't seem the type to be interested in spending the night with a stranger."

She's not.

"I'm usually not the type to sit in the tavern and speak to a stranger for hours either."

You're definitely not.

"So, you're saying you've already bent your rules for me?"

"I wouldn't call them rules," I flashed him a smile. His reciprocating one made my heart melt in ways I didn't think would ever be possible again. I couldn't help but wonder how his lips would feel against my own. He must have caught me staring at his full lips, he licked his own as he brought a hand to my face, lightly stroking my cheek with his finger. The touch of his hand sent electricity across my skin, goosebumps creeping over every inch of me.

"I had a hard time letting you leave earlier, and even after you've graced me with your company, I find myself even more hesitant to let you walk out that door. Please, stay?" His finger glided under my chin, his face edging closer to my own. Our lips were a breath apart.

I swallowed, I couldn't deny I didn't feel the same. But the thought of being with someone even with the hallucination of Maël always in my head didn't seem right.

You need to move on from me Alora.

But we were...

I can't love you like I once did. Please, stay.

I could feel Maël's presence recede into the dark depths, it reminded me of all the times we've ever walked away from each other. Just out of reach, yet never too far from one another.

I brought my focus back to the man before me. There was something about him that was so magnetic, infectious, that I couldn't help but stay and speak with him, to get to know him. I was a moth drawn to his flame. I nodded my head. He smiled and stood, taking my hands with his as he quietly led us up the stairs. I heard Evangeline giggling somewhere in the tavern below.

Ryn brought us to the room towards the end of the hall, using the old bronze key to open it.

"After you," he held his arm out through the doorway.

I stepped inside, Jones didn't keep these rooms quite to Vanya's standards but they were cozy. A fire blazed in the far corner, while a made bed awaited with a small pile of quilts. Before I could decide whether to take up one of the chairs near the fireplace or perch upon the bed, Ryn shut the door and spun me until my back hit the rough surface. His hand still holding the knob now beside my hip, the other braced above my head as he leaned into me. He kissed his way up the column of my neck, stopping near my ear.

"Did I tell you how devastatingly beautiful you are?" His breath tickled my ear.

I wrapped my arms around his neck, turning my face to meet his, "You may have mentioned that before your rant about how amazing you are." He chuckled before capturing my lips with his. The kiss was softer than I expected, until it wasn't. His hand came behind my neck, tilting my head back allowing his tongue to coax my mouth open for him. Tasting me. I felt a tug towards him, yet his hands didn't move. As if my very essence was wrapping itself around him as he claimed my mouth harder. The kiss deepened, causing me to gasp as I ran out of breath. As much as I was desperate for the oxygen, I couldn't wait more than a second before melding back into him.

Ryn let out a deep growl as his hands slid down to my hips, then gripping my ass until he lifted me into his arms. My legs wrapped around his torso. He turned, bringing us to the bed and laying me before him. His blue eyes trailed the length of my body as he began unlacing my boots. I sat up and pulled my tunic over my head, the cold air causing my nipples to pebble. With a thud from my boots hitting the ground, he shucked his own tunic, bearing his chiseled chest to me. I assessed him hungrily, the man was built like a fae god. A sun tattoo covered the left side of his chest, light blonde hair lightly trailing down towards the V that guided my eyesight towards the growing bulge in his leathers, laces already undone. He smirked catching my gaze, hooking his thumbs beneath his pants to push them down.

"Eyes on me, Love," He commanded me as he peeled my own leathers from my body. I bit my lip as he knelt before me, placing my heels on either side of him at the edge of the bed. He pulled his hair from its last remnants of the bun and it cascaded towards his broad shoulders as he settled himself between my legs, hands pushing each thigh further apart. I held his gaze as he took his tongue and licked down my center, teasing my entrance. With every stroke of his tongue my body became alight with pleasure. Crying out as he took the bundle of nerves in his mouth. I tangled my hands in his long hair, giving up on maintaining eye contact as he had me barreling towards the edge. He slid a finger inside me, then two as he continued his assault on my clit.

"You're so wet, Love," he pulled his fingers from me and sucked my juices off them, giving a satisfied groan. He fisted himself. He rubbed his hard length through my slick cunt. He curled a finger towards me, "Come taste how sweet you are."

I tried not to audibly gulp. I've never touched a man other than that last night with Maël. I was out of my element with this man. I would be mortified to have my inexperience ruin this moment.

I crawled to him, looking up at his handsome face through my lashes as I brought my lips towards his length. He said to taste...I bent down, sticking my tongue out and pressing it against his skin. Tasting his skin and myself as I licked up his shaft. A hand tangled in my hair as I met his bulbous head and he guided himself into my mouth. I almost choked as he pushed towards the back of my throat, drool dripping from my lips.

"Just relax," he encouraged. I relaxed my jaw open, giving him more room to slide further in. I instinctively closed my lips around him, sucking him, moving my tongue around him.

He groaned as his hold on me tightened, "Just like that, such a good girl." He began to pump into my mouth, moving his hips faster with every thrust as I tried to keep up. "Is that greedy cunt of yours ready for my cock, Love?"

Ryn pulled his cock from my mouth and wiped a bit of drool off my chin with his thumb as he moved us further up the hard mattress, climbing on top of me. He peppered my body with kisses as he nestled between my thighs, lining himself up with my entrance. He wrapped his arms around me as he eased into me, working each inch until he's fully sheathed.

"Ryn—" I cried, my fingers wrapped in his golden strands again as he completely filled me. Stars formed behind my eyes as he thrust steadily. My body shook, is this what real pleasure is? It felt like my very essence was melding with his. I started falling over the edge, wave after wave of ecstasy crashing through me as I lost myself in the feeling of him.

I didn't think it was possible, but I felt him harden even more. The feel of his solid length sliding to that perfect spot prolonged my orgasm as he chased his own release. Claiming my mouth. I didn't think I could feel fuller until he was pumping his seed deep inside me.

When we finally untangled ourselves from each other, he went to the wash room, his absence making my heart sink. When he returned, he had a damp cloth that he used to clean the mess between my legs. The soft, caring touch more familiar to the warm man I met downstairs than the ruthless one who claimed me. He stopped as he looked at the cloth, a tinge of red smeared on it.

"You should've told me I was your first, I would've taken more care to be gentle." He looked at me worried, like he broke me.

I shrugged, soreness starting to creep through my body, "I didn't mind." The way he stared, as if something was on his mind. Awkwardness began to settle into me like a dark cloak. He asked me to stay with him, but now that he's gotten what he wanted, did he want me to leave? I recalled how it felt to be held by him, kissed by him. Connecting him felt like a missing piece of me slid into place. Was I just being naive?

I swallowed my shame, trying to keep my voice from shaking, "Right, I guess I'll see you around." I pushed off the bed but he grabbed my wrist gently.

"Where are you going?" His eyes flicked between mine, confusion lining his face.

"I'm sorry, I thought—" I looked towards my clothing littering the floor and the door.

"Come back to bed, Love," he spoke without hesitation. "Unless you truly want to leave. I won't stop you, but I'd rather you stay." He let out a low laugh. "I'll beg you if I must."

Maybe I'm not alone with what I felt. As crazy as it seemed, there was something about Ryn that kept me entranced by him. The thought of leaving him here made my stomach churn, I'm not sure if my body would've let me physically do it.

With a soft smile, I slipped beneath the covers, his strong body curved around mine like a shield, his arms wrapping around me with a possessive tenderness. For the first time in years, peace settled over me like a warm blanket, pushing back the shadows of my blood-soaked past. That night, my dreams weren't filled with ash and death—with Maël and my grandmother burning before my eyes. Instead, I dreamed of golden light and warmth.

CHAPTER 25

Sunlight filtered through the dusty window, rousing me from slumber. A part of me still clung to disbelief, but the unfamiliar surroundings and the delicious ache between my thighs confirmed that last night had been gloriously real.

Never had I imagined I'd find myself here, savoring memories of a night wrapped in strong arms until dawn.

I stretched languidly, reaching out across the soft sheets, only to find cold emptiness where Ryn's warmth should have been. The heavy quilt slipped down as I bolted upright, scanning the empty chamber. Silence reigned, no sounds of life from the washroom. My gaze fell to the floor, where Ryn's discarded clothing should have been. Nothing. Not a single trace of him remained.

Foolish girl, I berated myself. *What did you expect?* I'd allowed myself to believe in that spark between us, to imagine last night was more than a fleeting moment of passion. All the while, he'd been plotting his escape, waiting for my guard to drop.

I sprang from the bed, my bare feet slapping against the cold wooden floors. I snatched up my scattered clothing, yanking it on haphazardly. My hands flew to my pockets, fingers closing around the familiar shape of my dagger and the comforting weight of my coin purse.

Not a common thief after all, I thought with a bitter laugh. *No, he'd claimed a far more precious prize—the heart I'd sworn to guard.*

The clamor from the tavern below drifted up the stairs, a cacophony of morning revelry. My stomach churned at the thought of facing Jones and Evangeline. As far as they knew, I'd slipped away in the dead of night.

Again, my mind is brought right back to the scene of last night's passion. The way Ryn had commanded me, his touch dominating every inch of my body, coaxing tremors of pleasure that bordered on pain.

I cursed my own foolishness. How could I have believed he wanted anything more than a quick tumble? It was always the same with guards in taverns. I'd witnessed it countless times, deflected countless propositions.

Since losing Maël, I'd kept my heart under lock and key. No man could hold a candle to the light he'd brought into my life. Until Ryn.

He'd pursued me relentlessly, coaxing words from my reluctant lips. I'd found myself sharing fragments of my life, hanging on every morsel he offered in return.

His smile had been radiant, as if he'd swallowed the sun itself. If ever there was a sun blessed being, it was him.

I heaved a sigh, padding silently toward the window. Dawn was breaking, but shadows still clung to the corners, offering me a chance at a stealthy escape.

I didn't bother with my hair, no doubt a tangled mess. The shadows I summoned would hide that embarrassment, at least. But they could do nothing for the shame burning in my chest.

I eased the window open, slipping out into the cool morning air. Gratitude washed over me. Second floor. A manageable drop, unlike the dizzying heights of the upper rooms.

Hugging the buildings, I glided past unsuspecting townsfolk like a wraith. Occasionally, I'd drift close enough for them to feel the air shift, their heads whipping around in confusion. To them, I was nothing more than a trick of the light, indistinguishable from their own shadows.

A year of wandering had etched the path from manor to tavern into my memory. Another six months before I could navigate the reverse without getting lost.

Miles slipped away beneath my feet until, finally, home loomed before me. Tall iron gates stood sentinel, a familiar welcome.

As I crossed the threshold, the morning's revelations began to loosen their stranglehold. I dismissed my shadows, drinking in the sight of ancient trees dotting the yard. Centuries-old giants, they towered over even the manor itself.

Vanya had once confided that these trees were why she'd chosen this place. A private forest with the conveniences of town nearby. I chuckled, recalling how my master's eyes had sparkled, her usual tough facade slipping. A woman wild enough to long for the forest, yet still covet her diamonds and silks.

Love. The voice exploded in my mind, frantic and desperate. My body thrummed with energy as I dropped into a crouch, hands flying to my temples. *Where did you go? Why did you leave?*

An onslaught of questions battered my mind. My throat constricted, pain lancing through me with each frenzied word.

Please, stop, I begged. In my mind's eye, I conjured a door, wide open to the voice. With all my might, I slammed it shut. Imaginary Maël appeared at my side, throwing his weight against the heavy wood until the lock clicked, silencing the intruder.

Who was that? Maël's voice was a whisper as I straightened, shaking off the lingering buzz.

I was hoping you could tell me, I replied, fighting back tears. But of course, figments of imagination rarely offer logical answers. Maël's presence faded, leaving me alone in the echoing chambers of my mind.

As I entered the manor, silence reigned, broken only by Cook's clamor in the kitchen.

Not ready to face the chatterbox, I made my way up the grand staircase, my fingers idly grazing the bannister.

"Well look what the cat dragged in," a voice purred from my left. Vanya emerged from the hallway opposite from where my room was. She halted before me, arms crossed and eyes narrowed. Any hope I had of her not hearing about last night evaporated.

"Follow me." She spun on her heel, leading me down the hall she came from. We passed door after door. I wondered how many others were home, if they'd eavesdrop on my impending reprimand. I groaned inwardly. Last night, I'd messed up in more ways than one. While I did neutralize the target, I made a scene. I let my own personal vendetta get in the way of all my training. That fallout led me to drown my woes in a tankard of ale, and we all know how well that turned out.

Vanya led me past her room, to the double doors that stood at the end of the hall. Thick wooden doors, carved with intricate swirls and patterns. She pushed the door open, gesturing for me to enter. She closed them behind us with a soft click as we stood in her office.

"Sit." She directed me to a chair as she rounded the desk and sat in her oversized leather seat. The back came above her head as she placed her elbows on the desk, her head drooping into her hands to rub her temples.

"Do you recall the meaning of discreet?" She inquired.

"Is this a trick question?" I almost laughed, but the exasperated look on her face stopped me. I cleared my throat and looked down at my hands, twisting my fingers together nervously. "I didn't intend to attract attention."

"And yet you did. Tell me, what possessed you to be so reckless? You are a literal shadow, practically invisible in the cover of darkness."

Because she can't let things go, your honor. Gods, he's back and sassier than ever.

"Tyrian gave chase after we engaged him. I didn't mean to make a spectacle, but I very well couldn't just let him get away."

"No, and thankfully you didn't." She sat back, eyes assessing me like she was trying to solve a puzzle. "Why didn't you cloak yourself?"

Confusion flashed in my eyes. I'd engaged my powers during the mission. It was rare that I didn't. "I was hidden, the only thing anyone could've noticed was a shadow. And given the fact that everyone has one of those it's not like I would've stood out."

I recalled the entire ordeal, telling her how I saw Johan in the middle of the chase. Up until Tyrian met his end in the alley.

To her credit, she listened to every word, her face morphing from annoyance to understanding, her mouth pressed in a tight line.

"I received a report that someone saw you," she explained. "Well who they believe you to be. I believe the exact words 'a short skinny male in all black'. Whatever you did with your," she waved her hand toward me, "power, someone was able to see you enough to tell the difference between a shadow and a person." She took some papers out from her desk as well as two pouches of coin. "Of course, there were plenty other accounts that Death's Wraith had struck again. As for the captain, I had planned to give you an update on my search for him when you returned, but it seems you preferred other... company."

I groaned. "I would have much preferred coming home."

She laughed, "I don't know, I heard he was pretty handsome, and you were smitten."

He was a handsome fellow, not near as ruggedly handsome as I am though.

I gawked at her. I could feel a blush creeping across my cheeks as I shifted uncomfortably in my seat. Part of me wasn't surprised Vanya knew, but knowing Maël was aware of my night with Ryn made me feel...unfaithful. Embodiment of my imagination or not.

No one could compare to you, Maël. You were always the one I chose.

It's time to choose someone else Alora. The sassy tone now gone as he spoke softly to me. *I want you to fall in love again and live the life you always dreamed of. Even if it's not with me. You have to let me go.*

As long as I draw breath Maël, I could never let you go.

He sighed, his presence in my mind beginning to recede once again, *you'll doom yourself Lor.*

"I have eyes everywhere, as one of them you should be well aware of that." She clipped, bringing my attention back to our lovely debrief. "Anyway, dear old Johan was in town last night, as you noticed, but he's since departed. Lucky for you, I know where he's heading." She tossed both pouches towards me, landing in a soft thump on the wooden desk.

"I'm reassigning you to the capital. I have a contact there you can pose as their employee. They have a spare room above their shop where you can sleep. It's not what you're used to, but I think you'll be able to help them and find what you seek."

While becoming a professional assassin wasn't what I had always dreamed of, it's become my life, my identity. I put in a lot of effort these past years honing my skill, pushing my powers further, helping Vanya rid the area of the corrupted that flocked to this near lawless town. The guards never cared about the victims, but Vanya did. Her clients were happy to invest in her services to wipe another speck of dirt off the face of this world. Learning the backstory of our targets helped me release the guilt of murdering them, with Vanya's help, I became what I sought out to be. An angel delivering retribution, I was vengeance. "Is this your way of kicking me out of the guild?"

"Your home will always be here Lor, you're my protege after all."

A reassuring smile brightened her face, "We both know your path is towards Johan. You're of more use at the capital, chasing him and sending me any intel you can dig up while you're there. And when you're done, I'd like nothing more than for you to return here and help me run the guild. As of today, I'm officially naming you my heir. Whether you come back or not," she stretched her arms in grandeur, "this is all yours. I hope you ensure our mission continues even when some poor soul manages to get a cheap shot off me."

I shook my head and returned her smile, "You know I will. Though I expect your ornery ass to be around for a long time. What does this friend of yours do exactly? Smuggler? It's your creepy diamond dealer isn't it?"

"Evander is not creepy!" She shrieked with delight, "Just lacks good people skills. No, you won't be working for him if that's what you're worried about. I'm sure you'll be thrilled."

I waited for her to grace me with the information I asked for, with a roll of her eyes she scribbled something on the paper before her before handing it over. They're detailed directions. A sly smile stretched across her face.

"You'll report to the bookshop in the square within a few days. Raven's ready for you in the stables, stay on the path heading South. It will take you straight to the capital and if you stay on it you'll find yourself in the center square. There's a big obnoxious statue of the king, there's no way you can miss it."

A bookshop! This was fitting of the dreams I had long ago. "What are these for?" I pointed at the pages she had given me.

"A plan B if you don't listen to me and stray off the path. Ensure you don't need them." She said sternly. "Now go fix that bird's nest you call hair and head out. I expect you to keep me updated, if you find you need anything let Augustus know or myself."

We both stood, clasping hands across the desk. Her eyes filled with pride as she gave me one final once over.

"Thank you." I felt tears threaten to emerge from my eyes. I didn't think leaving, even temporarily, would feel so hard. But this quickly became home, Vanya was like the mother I never got to know.

"Destiny only calls those courageous enough to stare her in the face. You, my dear, are one of the most valiant assassins to ever cross this threshold." With a final squeeze of her hand, she released mine. Standing tall, chin raised, "Hurry along, Augustus is expecting you in a few days and he's got an aversion for tardiness."

I nodded, my legs swiftly guiding me out of the room. I felt distant from my body as I cleaned up and donned fresh clothes and gathered my things. Looking at my bookshelf where I began collecting the books I always longed for, I grabbed my old favorite, the one I carried with me from the village. My eyes caught the blue leather of the history book gifted to me by that kind old man long ago. I never got around to reading it, history was never my favorite subject, opting for romances and tales of adventure. I picked it up and added it to my pack, maybe it will help while I'm in a place filled with Sunneva's history. Finding myself content, I left Lucas a note on his door, promising to write once I arrived. As I headed towards the stables, I couldn't help but hold my head high. Johan may have gotten away from me, but I was ready for a hunt. He just didn't know he was the deer.

CHAPTER 26

I heed Vanya's words and stick to the main road leading out of Bridgedale, heading south towards the capital. I recalled my journey from my former village to the little towns I spent my time simply surviving in. The memories weighed heavy in my chest, each step forward a reminder of how far I'd come from those desperate days. Then that final journey to Bridgedale. I skulked through the woods, trying not to attract any attention, afraid of robbers or worse. Now, I rode with my head held high.

Raven, my trusty companion, was happy to be out of the stable. When I found us alone, I would pull shadows to us, practicing covering myself plus an extension. Raven didn't seem to mind when the inky tendrils surrounded him, it was like he felt at one with the darkness. Or maybe he enjoyed the extra treats I gave him throughout the day. Either way, the day Vanya had gifted him to me was one of the happiest since finding the guild. My soul had found a kindred spirit in the animal and he seemed to have agreed the same for him.

One night, I lit a fire and created a wall of shadow around us. The power thrummed through my veins like liquid night. Testing my limits, I stretched the shadows to cover just my steed. The firelight transformed him into something otherworldly, rising from the dark depths of hell, the shadows giving him a dark ethereal presence, tendrils leeching out from him like a black flame. Even without shadow magic, my mount was magnificent, but the sight of him made me awestruck. Together, we were creatures of darkness and shadow.

In these quiet moments, I sensed Raven understood me in ways no human ever had. He wasn't just accepting my shadows; he was embracing them, becoming one with them, as if the magic had woven an unbreakable thread between our souls. Each time the darkness enveloped him, his trust in me grew stronger, and with it, my confidence in wielding this newfound power. We were no longer just rider and mount, but partners in this dance of shadow and night.

The shadow barrier held through the night, but exhaustion dragged at my bones until I could barely stay upright. Raven's steady gait seemed to stretch time like molasses. The world blurred at the edges, my muscles trembling with each league we covered, while shadows seemed to dance mockingly at the corners of my vision.

Epherinia loomed just a day's ride away. I should have been thrilled. A life among endless shelves of books awaited me—a dream I'd barely dared to imagine. But my thoughts betrayed me, always circling back to Ryn, of the life I had allowed myself to desire even just for a moment. Gods, I had no right to miss him. I barely knew him. That morning had proven just how little I truly meant to him. I'd been naive to think the pull I felt was mutual. Even now, my heart ached from the separation, a physical pain that twisted in my chest like a dagger, making each breath a reminder of his absence.

"Pull yourself together," I muttered. Raven snorted in response, making it clear he thought I was being ridiculous while he remained the picture of perfection.

You're far from losing your mind, little hunter. The voice was warm and familiar, wrapping around my mind like a tender embrace, sending shivers down my spine. Maël's presence, even just in my thoughts, made my heart stutter.

Everything I thought I knew about myself is slipping away.

You're stronger than you know, Alora. This is just another step in your journey.

I stroked his neck and led him to the edge for a drink and knelt to refresh myself. The icy water soothed my overtaxed body and mind. I leaned back, fingers digging into soft grass, face turned skyward as if the sun could burn away my exhaustion.

A sniffle to my right caused me to whirl toward the bushes. My eyes narrowed as I caught a shift in the light. Something was in there. A whimper came from it this time as I stood. My fingers found the hilt of my blade. Those sounds were too human to be an animal, but could signal a trap. Even Raven seemed to go tense and silent as I took slow measured steps towards the bush. Once I came upon it, I looked over the top to see a little face peeking up at me. Dirt-streaked cheeks and tangled blonde hair greeted my eyes.

"What are you doing out here?" I asked, keeping my voice gentle.

The boy startled, his green eyes wide with fear as he scrambled backward from his leafy sanctuary.

"Please don't hurt me!" he cried, his voice trembling.

I shook my head. "I won't hurt you, little one. Are you alone? Where are your parents?"

He rose, wringing his small hands. Despite his dirt-streaked face and tangled hair, his clothes were pristine save for the mud caking his shoes.

"They don't know I'm here. I was playing with Billy," he sniffled, fighting back tears. "A-and I got lost. Please, I just want to go home."

My heart ached for him. Another lost child in the wilderness, like so many tragic stories I'd heard before.

I scanned the area, ensuring no ambush awaited us.

"Come on, I'll take you to Epherinia. The constable can help find your family." I extended my hand, offering a gentle smile.

He wiped his eyes, further smearing the dirt across his cheeks, and took my hand. "Thank you, kind lady."

"I couldn't leave you alone out here," I said, leading him to Raven.

The boy froze, gaping at my mount. Raven cut an imposing figure with his towering height and unflinching gaze.

Raven had been won from an old warlord, Vanya once told me. He was the kind of beast who never backed down.

Life in Vanya's stables had softened his war-hardened edges, but now, back on the road, he carried himself like the warrior he once was, his eyes bright with renewed purpose.

Adventure called to him as strongly as it called to me.

Raven lowered his head to investigate the boy, nosing at his pockets for treats. Finding none, he snorted his disappointment.

I knelt beside the child, retrieving a small biscuit from my pocket and pressing it into his tiny palm.

"What's your name?" I asked as he offered the treat to Raven, giggling when the steed's velvety lips brushed his palm to accept the bribe.

"My name's Davian." He pressed his palm just above Raven's nose. "Can I ride him?" His green eyes sparkled with hope as he looked up at me.

I laughed. "We're going to have to." Rising, I guided him to Raven's side, gripped his small hips, and lifted him into the front of the saddle. Once his hands clutched the horn, I swung up behind him, creating a protective circle with my arms as I took the reins. With a gentle nudge, I turned Raven back toward the path.

"What's your name, miss?" Davian twisted to look at me over his shoulder. The frightened child was gone, replaced by a bright-eyed boy vibrating with excitement. My chest tightened as I thought of his family.

His mother must be frantic, discovering her child missing. I pushed away thoughts of searching for Billy. I couldn't spare the time to look for another lost child. The one I'd found needed to return home quickly.

I ruffled his dirty hair, golden strands gleaming beneath the grime like his brilliant smile. "I'm Lor. Better hold tight. Raven loves the wind in his mane too much to stop for fallen riders."

I don't believe for a second he's the only one.

I laughed and urged Raven forward. Davian's knuckles went white on the horn, but his whoops of joy filled the air as if the threat of falling only made it more thrilling.

We reached Epherinia sooner than expected, crossing through the main gates as dawn painted the sky. After securing Raven in the city stables, we walked the main path until we faced an imposing statue. The crowned figure loomed above us, one hand resting on his sword's pommel, the other cradling a miniature sun. The king's likeness marked this as the square. Beyond his golden form, a shop window caught my eye, its display filled with books. I knocked on the door, praying the owner had arrived early.

"Can't you read the sign?" a gruff voice called from within. "We don't open for another—"

The door swung open to reveal the old man who had tended my wounds after Donovan's torture. His weathered face broke into an instant smile.

"It's you!" His gaze dropped to Davian, brows furrowing. "And who's this? Your child?" His eyes darted between us, searching for shared features.

"I found him during my journey. Could you help us contact a guard? He needs to return to his family." The old man nodded, beckoning us inside.

"Up those stairs, lad. Get yourself cleaned up while we sort this out." Davian bounded up the steps behind the desk, eager to wash away the evidence of his ordeal.

"You never mentioned knowing Vanya. Just who are you?" I studied the old man's face.

"You never asked. Would it have mattered? You needed a place in the capital, and I needed help." His gesture encompassed the chaos of his bookstore.

"You certainly do." The shop was indeed in disarray, stacks and stacks of books waiting to be placed on a shelf or displayed on a table. The desk was littered with parchments. How the old man functioned was beyond me.

He stepped behind me to a small kitchen in the back of the place, making a small plate of food and setting it on the wooden table. Soft steps came down the stairs as Davian returned, sans dirt.

"Well well well, there is a cute face under there after all. Wouldn't even know I found you crying in a bush." I cooed.

He began wolfing down his food, barely pausing between bites, "I would rather not talk about my tears. I'm twelve and still act like a baby." His voice dropped, shame coloring his words.

"Hmm, I don't know," I mused. "Not many twelve year olds would've had the courage to stay alive, let alone face Raven. He prides himself in the fear he strikes in others."

"He's a big softie. I doubt others are afraid of him," Davian scoffed.

I recalled the weary looks Raven drew from passing travelers, and even the stable hand earlier. The young man had turned white when he saw Raven, and my mount had fixed him with that predatory stare.

"Trust me, he strikes fear in the hearts of others. Your courage knows no bounds, Davian."

Davian shot me a smile, his face brightening. "Thank you for finding me."

Warmth bloomed in my chest as I watched him. Truly, I was thankful to have found him, sparing him from a night alone in the wilderness. Our short time together reminded me what it meant to truly help someone... without a murder being involved, at least. These past years my form of help had meant unlawful means. It was refreshing to do something so humble.

"Anytime you need anything, come find me. I'll always come, maybe Raven too," I promised.

The bell above the door chimed and Augustus entered with the guard. The moment the guard laid eyes on Davian, recognition flashed across his face, and a sigh escaped him.

"C'mon boy, let's get you home before your mother has another one of her episodes." Davian stood up and went to the man without another word. The guard and Augustus exchanged a nod, and with that they left.

As Davian looked over his shoulder one last time before stepping through the doorway, I sent him an encouraging nod. Once they disappeared, I slumped in my seat. An unexpected ache of loss hit me as I missed the little rascal.

CHAPTER 27

My first week at the bookshop passed quickly. Augustus wasn't as gruff as he seemed, just impatient. I restocked shelves, dusted, and helped customers by day. At night, I prowled the capital's square, searching for traces of Johan before returning to my apartment above the store. The memories of the manor, what was now home, hit like a blade between my ribs. Missing it was like a physical wound. From the bustle of the manor's kitchen to the guys as they told their tales from their most recent jobs. I missed Lucas egging someone on in a bet. Half the time, Vanya would sway drunkenly on the tables, stirring up a dance and dragging anyone she could get her hands on to join her.

I penned a coded update for the guild master, ink blooming across rough parchment. Between the whispers around town and my search for the old captain, I had plenty to hide beneath clever phrases. Afternoon sun streamed through dusty windows as I worked, surrounded by the scent of old books and leather. I spotted ladies approaching and swiftly hid the sealed letter under my book - "The History of the Sun, Moon, and Stars." The dry text revealed useful details about Sunneva: the king's bloody rise to power after his uncle's coup, and Epherinia's advanced aqueduct system that boosted crop yields. Though less exciting than my usual romances, I stored away these facts for later use.

"Welcome, is there anything I can help you find today?"

One of them, a petite blonde with golden ringlets tumbling down her shoulders, looked up at me with a smile, "Do you have any poetry books?"

"We do, here, let me show you." I led them over to a shelf along the larger wall. "Is there a particular poetry book you're looking for?"

The blonde's companion, a tall woman with honeyed skin and dark hair coiled elegantly atop her head, eyed me with suspicion, "I've never seen you around before. Are you new?"

I fought the urge to roll my eyes. Within seconds, I had already figured her out. I flashed a meek smile and feigned nervousness. "I am. I've just arrived to help my uncle with his shop. How about this one?" I plucked a poetry book filled with saccharine romantic limericks and held it out to the blonde.

"Oh this looks lovely!" She squealed. She flipped through the pages, with each sampling her smile grew. "This is perfect. I'll take it."

Her friend didn't say another word as I rang her up at the counter and wrapped her book in brown parchment.

"Come back soon!" I told them as I handed the woman her new collection of poetry.

"We will! It was so lovely to meet you," the blonde gushed. "You'll have to join us for tea one afternoon." After a pause, she lightly elbowed her friend to speak.

"Yes," she sounded reluctant, "you simply must join us."

"That would be delightful," I replied with a practiced smile, though my insides twisted at the thought. Like bile rising in my throat, the memory of my last ladies' tea in Bridgedale surfaced. Hours of mindless chatter while I posed as an attendee, watching my target drone on about her latest silk purchases. That particular job had almost been compromised when I choked back rage along with my tea. When darkness fell and my blade found its mark, I felt nothing. Between the mind-numbing facade and the children she'd sold into darkness, my humanity had taken a necessary pause, a mercy I hadn't extended to her.

When the shop door finally closed behind them, I released a breath I hadn't realized I'd been holding. The whole interaction felt wrong, like donning another's skin. I was made for shadows and silence, for gathering secrets unseen. Not this bright, chattering world of pleasantries that left me hollow.

After dusting spines meticulously, I organized the counter. Augustus would return soon with his usual flood of papers. I left my letter and his mail on his desk - the only spot he'd notice things needed sending.

The door chimed again and in came Augustus with a portly man who persisted in speaking.

"...I know you don't believe but she *must* come and be tested. The king's will demands it. As his herald, I must insist—"

"Yes, yes, Shefferd," Augustus waved him off and through the door. "We'll arrive tomorrow for the lunacy of your test. I expect payment for the time my shop is closed, wasted on such fallacies."

Shefferd bowed. "Of course, the crown is happy to oblige." His chest puffed with self-importance as he scurried away, practically preening at his successful errand.

Augustus's dark grey hair caught the afternoon light, silver threading through the strands. He surveyed the shop with a critical eye, nodding in satisfaction and continued towards the back office.

"How many customers did you scare away today, lass?" he asked with a chuckle.

"I'll have you know, I haven't scared off a single customer since I've arrived," I retorted. "What was that all about?"

"Aye, we're to present ourselves at the palace tomorrow. The king demands some sort of assessment." He dismissed the subject with a wave of his hand as he passed me. "What about the young men who have swiftly walked out after setting their sights on you?"

I rolled my eyes. "I can hardly be blamed for that. All I did was smile and welcome them. Now tell me more about this assessment."

Though lacking Vanya's grandeur, his presence commanded the same respect as he settled into his wooden chair. "Power-hungry fools, the lot of them. The king is convinced there's a powerful match for his son, the older prince. This test is how he seeks this so-called match—it's nothing but a waste of time. The crown's always meddling where they shouldn't, taking time from honest merchants. But business is business, so would it kill you to smile, maybe flirt with them a little? Just enough to get them to buy something."

"Would you rather I scowl and throw a dagger at them? That can be easily arranged, and frankly preferred since I'd have more time to read."

"You can't blame them for being curious about a new face in town. Back then, every suitor came bearing flowers."

"I can blame them," I said, jaw clenched. "I'm not interested in anything other than what I came here to do." The weight of my mission pressed against my chest, but curiosity softened my voice. "Is that how you met your wife? By bringing her a rose?"

"No, no," he said, a ghost of a smile playing at his lips, "I brought her a sunflower," he said, pride warming his voice. "I spoke to her sister and found out they were her favorite."

"How many sunflowers did she receive?"

"One," he said softly, lost in the memory. "No one else thought to ask." His voice cracked slightly as he looked down at his desk, busying his hands with the papers.

CHAPTER 28

"Remember, in and out. Do whatever the mage asks of you. Stay quiet, and for gods' sake, do not get snarky with them." Augustus urged me along the path towards the palace.

"Act like a mute, obedient damsel who doesn't have a single thought of her own, got it." The comment earned me a sharp look from the old man.

Every man's fantasy.

Oh, is that what you pictured when you thought of me as a wife?

No, I knew what I was getting myself into, you are more than enough as you are.

"This would be much easier if you were actually mute."

"You know, I could have come myself. You didn't need to close the shop for the day."

"The butcher's shop is literally two blocks from the shop." He peered at me over the rim of his glasses.

I rolled my eyes. So I got a little turned around after taking a detour? I always tried to get in some scouting during my errands, plus I still made it back.

As we approached the massive doors of the gilded palace, I took in the front gardens. The grounds sprawled before us, meticulously maintained and adorned with a sun on practically every surface.

Augustus presented our names to the guards flanking the entrance, and they waved us through.

"Ah, perfect timing! Come along, their majesties await." Shefferd bustled us through the grand hall past the open doors before us. "What was your name again?"

"Alora," I replied.

My heart stuttered in my chest as my gaze collided with familiar blue eyes. Ryn. Raw surprise flashed across his features before anger darkened his expression. His jaw clenched, the muscles working beneath sun-kissed skin as his fingers dug into the gilded throne arms. The air grew thick with tension, charged with unspoken accusations and hurt.

I scanned the room as we approached the dais where a small crowd had gathered. I recognized almost no one, but I did spot the two women who came to the shop. My stomach twisted at their presence, a bitter reminder of how this mess began.

Surely the royal family had more pressing matters than watching some shopkeeper's niece perform a magical test. Something wasn't adding up. The pieces of this puzzle refused to align.

Beside the queen sat another prince on a smaller throne. His cheeks flushed as he studied his hands. Davian mirrored his mother's features perfectly, now that I saw them together. He glanced up, catching my gaze with a half-smile before returning to his carefully maintained invisibility. No wonder the guard had been so eager to return him home—he wasn't just some lost village boy after all. The queen would have razed the realm to the ground to bring her son home.

"Your Grace," Shefferd cleared his throat. "I present to you Augustus Denarius and his niece Alora. They have come to complete the assessment."

The king nodded then movement stirred from the right of the dais. An old woman stepped forward, a crystal orb held in her hands. Her sleek white hair was intricately woven around a crystal headdress, equally white eyes stared at me, they might even have been looking through me.

"I am Elvirana, Royal Mage of the Crown. I stand before you today to test your power. A tale from long ago has foretold of a powerful match for our kingdom. May we find the sun blessed match to bring victory to Sunneva." The small crowd erupted in cheers at the thought of the end of the war. She held the orb towards me. I looked to Augustus who had a masked expression, silently urging me to get this over with so we could return to our normal routine. "Place your hands on the orb girl. Show me your power."

I looked at the crystal sphere before me. It didn't appear threatening. Those eery white eyes along with everyone else stared at me. The king and queen looked annoyed at my hesitance. Ryn still glared daggers at me. It was tempting to launch one of the daggers sheathed in my leggings at his stupid handsome face, but I had promised Augustus I would behave.

I took a deep breath and placed my hand on the orb. At first, it was cool to the touch as my fingertips made contact. Once my full palm lay flat on its surface, a heat began to build, pulsing from it, up my arm, and into my chest. A pulse matched my heartbeat. For a moment, I was no longer in the throne room but in the woods just outside my childhood village. My grandmother walked before me, chanting words I did not recognize.

"Runerth must be found...may the starlight bless you...peace will come when a Satori sits on a throne of stars..."

I was only picking up a few words and missing many in between. I didn't feel in control of my body as I followed behind her. The same phrase repeating, the same pieces missing until I was suddenly pulled back before the old mage. I was not sure if it was this eerie ordeal or her lifeless eyes, but when she smiled it felt sinister, an inkling of dread twisting around my gut.

"You are Sun Blessed." She turned to the now excited king and nodded before disappearing around the dais, leaving me utterly confused. Augustus looked pale as I tried to piece together what just happened.

The king stood from his throne, pride swelling in his chest. "The day we've long awaited has finally come. A powerful match has been made, may this lead us towards our victory in the war with the North. We shall hold a ball in a week's time in honor of Prince Oryn's betrothal." He held his hand out for his wife, who took it and grabbed her young son, and they departed.

Shefferd began speaking to Augustus as my eyes found the clear blue of Ryn's. His earlier anger had transformed into pure fury. He stared me down with narrowed eyes for a moment longer and I felt my breath catch. He stormed away after his parents, and I was left alone with my "uncle" and the hand. The attendees filed out now that the spectacle was over.

Maël... I felt as if I were about to have a panic attack. My vision threatened to blacken as I tried to control my breathing.

I know, Alora, but this gives you a better opportunity to get the intel Vanya needs.

Fuck Vanya's intel, I didn't sign up to marry a prince.

A prince you've already bedded. He's not bad on the eyes—it could be worse.

Oh right, he could HATE me, which, by the way he looked at me, he does.

Love and hate often blur.

"...She will need to move into the palace immediately. We will send an escort for her belongings."

I snapped my head toward the two men wrapped in their discussion.

"She should return with me—it's not proper for her to live under the same roof as her...betrothed...before they marry." Augustus pulled at strings to get me out of here.

"I assure you, Denarius, she will be looked after with the utmost care. No one would dare harm her within the palace walls, and the king simply won't allow her to roam without proper protection."

Augustus let out a laugh. "You mean he doesn't want to risk her running away?"

"Are you suggesting your niece would commit treason by running from her duty?" Shefferd lifted an eyebrow at the bookkeeper.

"My uncle only jests. I would never consider turning my back on the crown and am honored to fulfill my duties to it." I answered. "May I have a moment with my uncle? Please?"

Shefferd obliged, "I'll be just outside the doors when you're ready for a tour. We'll get you settled in and send someone with your uncle for your things." He left us without another thought. Once we remained the only two in the room, I turned towards Augustus.

"You have time to run—I can distract them."

"If I run, they'll come after you, and I can't do that." Augustus began to argue but my attention was captured by a man who walked by the open doors speaking to a guard. He didn't even look my way, but I would have recognized his face anywhere. After all, he had plagued my nightmares every night for years. Captain Johan whispered to the guard as they passed, unaware of the reaper who was now locked on his every move.

"Lor?" Augustus' voice brought me back as Johan disappeared from view.

"Johan is here." My voice dropped to a whisper. "Send my things, but keep my items safe. I'll retrieve them myself."

Augustus nodded, recognizing the deadly promise in my words.

"And this marriage business?"

I shrugged, "Prince Oryn didn't seem thrilled about it. If I can get to Johan before the wedding, then there's not much left for me here." I looked at the old man. "Can you get to Bridgedale before then?"

"They'll expect the only family they're aware of to attend, and I'm not leaving you here alone, kid."

"We all must play our parts, Uncle." His eyes softened at the sentiment. "Promise me you'll leave after the ball. When I vanish, they'll seek retribution, and I won't let you become their target. I owe Vanya my life—I won't repay that debt by leading her brother to the executioner's block."

His brows pulled to a tight line. "How did you know?"

"Lucky guess—you guys look similar, have the same mannerisms but in different ways. The biggest tell was when you told me you were seeing your sister the night we met, and when I arrived, you introduced me as your niece to others."

"My sister never shortchanged your wit, lass." He pulled me into a hug; at first, I froze. Then I wrapped my arms around him and relaxed. "You're family to her, which means you're family to me. I'll stay for the ball. And I'll plan to stay with her shortly after. You better come back to us. Idiotic prophecies be damned, don't let yourself be a pawn in this madness of a war."

I pulled away and nodded, then walked with him back to the foyer where he departed, and I was left with Shefferd, the most joyous tour guide in all the land.

"How exciting it must be for you to marry the prince and aid in his victory." He crooned as he took me down hall after hall, barely stopping as he directed me to which room was which.

Yes, how exciting it was to be betrothed to a man I spent a night with, only to have him leave me by morning. I went along with the tour until I was deposited in my own room. The thrill of a hunt buzzed throughout my body. I could almost feel my blade sliding across Johan's throat—I just needed to survive long enough to see it through.

CHAPTER 29

When morning came, I found two deliveries waiting. The first contained my belongings from the apartment above the bookshop.

An aged trunk sat with my clothes and books. My fighting leathers and weapons were purposely absent. Someone had clearly searched through my possessions for contraband.

Augustus had included my two worn books, along with several other volumes. Among them were new romance novels I hadn't read yet. He'd also packed his precious history books about Sunneva. If he couldn't be here to help me, this was probably the next best thing he could do. His gesture spoke of a quiet, desperate hope that knowledge might protect me where he could not.

I wondered if any of these included information on the prophecy. Though knowing Augustus's views, these would likely contain only the crown-approved version of events.

I pulled one of the few simple dresses from the chest and changed out of the nightgown I'd worn to sleep. The morning light revealed the room's true grandeur, fit for the princess I was meant to become.

The four-poster bed had piles of cream and golden blankets atop it. Each spiral led up to a canopy of pink adorned with a sun. A marble fireplace commanded one wall, flanked by plush chairs.

Two glass doors led out to a small balcony, a promising escape route.

I made a mental note to watch the guard rotations and their sight lines to the balcony.

The wardrobe stood empty when I opened it.

I noted a couple of places that would be good for a weapons stash before placing my sparse belongings and closing the wooden doors. Another door caught my attention to the left of my bed.

As I went to open it, the handle didn't budge. I tried to force it, but still, it did not yield. There were no holes for me to attempt to pick the lock. My instincts screaming danger, I wedged a trinket from the mantle between the door and floor. If someone tried to enter, it would give me a second to act before I found myself a victim in someone else's schemes.

A knock at my door announced my second delivery. Oryn, his expression as murderous as yesterday. My body hummed with awareness as I stumbled back. He seized the opportunity, striding into the room and closing the door behind him.

"Who sent you?" he growled. My heart thundered against my ribs as I fought the urge to summon my shadows.

I arched a brow as he stalked toward me like a predator, his tall frame looming over me with a sneer.

"You expect me to believe this is coincidence?" he demanded, voice rough with hurt. "That we met, shared that night together before you vanished at dawn, cut off all communication, only to appear here as my chosen bride?"

I scoffed, my hands clenching at my sides. The audacity of him to accuse me when he'd been the one to disappear. Typical entitled prince.

"First of all," I snarled, "*I* didn't ditch *you*. That would require you actually being there. Secondly, I never chose any of this—not the assessment, not coming here, and certainly not marrying you."

I stumbled away from him to get some distance but he followed me step for step until he cornered me up against a wall. His arm slammed against the wall above me, the smell of citrus enveloped me.

"Is that why you left?" The look of murder eased from his eyes as his other hand toyed with a lock of my hair. "Because you awoke to an empty bed? Why didn't you just tell me when I tried to reach you through our bond? I felt you, heard you before you slammed that door shut."

"I have no idea what game you're playing, your message was loud and clear, Prince Oryn." I tensed as his hand drifted to caress my arm. I cursed myself for leaving my dagger by the bed. Even my shadows would be useless with him pressed so close. "You got what you wanted and promptly left by first light. I'm not sure why I expected anything differently from a *captain in a tavern.*"

He gripped my chin between his finger and thumb and forced me to look into his deep blue eyes. "I don't know what you *think* I wanted, but to return to you gone was not that." His words barely registered before his mouth crashed against mine, desperate and demanding. His hand slid to the front of my neck as his tongue coaxed my mouth to open further for him. The need to touch him overwhelmed me, pulling him closer until his entire body pressed me against the wall. That familiar buzz returned to a happy hum with every connection to the prince. How could I make sense of this? If he was upset I had left, if he had returned, why leave in the first place? My thoughts scattered like leaves in a storm. I was too lost in the feeling of him, almost drowning in him. The fog in my mind finally cleared enough for me to shove him away. He stared at me confused.

"If you didn't want me to leave, you should've been there. What else was I supposed to think when I woke up alone?"

He raked his hair from his face, taking a step away and faced the room. "I had duties to attend to. And I never thought my mate would flee at first light. I also didn't imagine the first time I used our bond to reach out that you'd cut it off." He paced slowly before me, his hands waving with flourish with every thought he spoke. "Did it ever occur to you I'd be back? Did you even think to wait for me? I was worried something happened to you."

His response made me pause. "What are you talking about? What do you mean our bond?"

"You're telling me you can't feel this pull between us?" He closes the distance between us, his presence overwhelming my senses.

"The way you call to me is maddening. I sought you everywhere yesterday. From the moment you walked into that tavern, nothing else existed but you. When you tried to leave that night, I meant every word about begging you to stay. The thought of you walking away felt like a blade twisting in my chest. Did you not hear me calling to you that morning?"

The pull to him was undeniable. Like a sickness in my blood since that night, making me speak more than I ever would, drawing me back for more time with him. The devastation when I woke alone had shattered something inside me. I wasn't imagining the voices of both him and Maël. Deep in my mind, my consciousness brushed against that door where I'd felt such insistent pounding before. Now only the faintest taps remained.

You should open it, Lor, Maël's voice floated to me like a gentle touch, distant but comforting.

I cracked open that mental barrier with trembling caution. A foreign presence rushed in immediately.

There you are, Love. I stared at Oryn's unmoving lips while his voice caressed my mind, intimate and impossible. My heart stuttered in my chest as ice flooded my veins, the reality of what this meant threatening to bring me to my knees.

"Has no one ever told you about mates?" His voice softened, he could sense the storm of emotions coursing through me as memories of our time together flooded back.

The fury in his eyes yesterday had cut deep, yet I couldn't look away from him. My isolated life in the village had left me ignorant of so much. I'd never witnessed a mated pair, never heard whispers of such an overwhelming connection. The pull between us bordered on madness.

In the days after our night together, thoughts of him haunted me like a sweet poison. I'd buried those feelings deep, locked them away where they couldn't torment me. I convinced myself I'd been nothing more than a conquest, a fool dancing to his tune. Yesterday's cold fury was a stark contrast to that night when he'd looked at me like I held all the stars in my hands.

He lifted his gaze to the ceiling, releasing a heavy breath before capturing my hands in his warm grip.

"Gods, I wanted to hate you. What else could I think when you vanished, when you rejected our bond?"

I never knew, I whispered through our newfound connection.

I understand now. His lips found mine before I could respond.

I melted into his kiss, savoring every brush of skin against skin as our bond sang between us.

Oryn drew away, resting his forehead against my own. "I'm sorry for not being there that morning, but I need you to know I had no intentions of ever parting from you once we met." His voice was low, laced with regret and sorrow.

I nodded, my mind reeling. The weight of this revelation settled over me like a heavy cloak. Betrothed. Mates. And my plans to vanish before becoming his wife. I couldn't afford to be drawn into his orbit, no matter how tempting.

"What does this mean?" I asked, my voice barely above a whisper. The words felt inadequate, but they were all I could muster in the face of this life-altering revelation.

Oryn's fingers found a lock of my hair, twirling it gently as he spoke. "To be mated?" His voice dropped low, as if sharing a secret. "There weren't many texts on the subject. Most are nearly as ancient as the prophecy itself. But I've always been told it's a bond like no other. You couldn't live and breathe without the other. Once sealed, it could never be broken." His eyes locked with mine, intense and unwavering. "Most accounts speak of the mind connection. It was the only way I could think to reach you." He paused, his words heavy with meaning. "There's no one else for me, Lor. The Gods themselves tied my fate to yours, and yours to mine. In this life and all the others after."

The truth crashed over me like a tidal wave. This man's fate, eternally bound to mine. A beautiful, terrifying prospect that threatened to unravel everything I'd planned.

"I need some space to process all of this." I lied. Every fiber of my being yearned to abandon my carefully laid plans for him. The bond called to me like a siren's song, but I couldn't yield. I had to see this through, Johan had to die and he was somewhere in this palace. If I could put enough space between us, maybe I could keep control long enough to finish my mission. Even if it meant hurting myself by limiting my time left with Ryn before I became nothing more than a murderess in his eyes.

He looked hurt but nodded in acceptance.

"I understand," he said softly. "We'll take this slowly, navigate through whatever festivities my mother has undoubtedly planned." "Will you allow me to call on you at least once a day? Since our bonding, the very thought of distance feels like agony." His voice carried the weight of sincerity, raw and vulnerable despite his royal bearing.

"I'd like that," I breathed, the words escaping before reason could catch them. The thought should have terrified me, but instead, his presence called to me like a flame to a moth. This bond was already proving to be a liability.

"Just promise you won't close that door again," he whispered, his gaze boring into mine with an intensity that sent my heart racing. "I won't hover, but being cut off from you... it's unbearable."

Could I hide the darkness that lurked beneath my skin? The secrets that would shatter everything between us?

Through our newly reopened bond, a golden cord that hummed between our souls. Our connection shimmered like starlight on water, delicate yet unbreakable.

"Only if you promise not to pry," I warned, though my attempt at sternness wavered beneath the radiance of his smile. The way he looked at me made my knees weak, as if he could see straight through to my soul. His beauty was a weapon I wasn't prepared to defend against.

"I promise, Love," he breathed, sealing his oath against my skin.

His lips brushed mine in a gentle kiss before he pulled away. "I'll see you at breakfast," he murmured against my lips, "and then I'll guide you through every secret this palace holds."

Shortly after, another knock echoed from the door. Before I could reach it, two women swept into the room uninvited.

"Hello Lady Alora," the older woman said with an artificially pleasant voice. "I'm Miss Gregoria, and I'm the Head of Household. I oversee the staff and will be managing your schedule." Like one of the stern matrons from my childhood fairytales come to life, she loomed tall and willowy before me.

Behind Miss Gregoria, a young woman with warm brown eyes offered a timid smile. Her arms cradled what appeared to be a dress. Her curly dark blonde hair was pulled back into a neat bun, a softer style than Miss Gregoria's austere arrangement.

The crone's lips pursed as her gaze raked over my dress, her disdain barely concealed. "Luella, please be sure Lady Alora is dressed appropriately for her meal. I'll see to it the dressmaker comes for a fitting this afternoon."

"Yes Miss Gregoria," Luella curtsies as the old woman departs. Once the door clicks shut, Luella raises her head to me. "Let me help you with this." She unfurls a stunning maroon gown, its gauzy fabric floating like blood in water. A far cry from my usual wardrobe. From beneath the dress, she produces a pair of slippers. The pale slippers shimmer with intricate patterns of gold thread and beads, like sunlight captured in silk. "Her Majesty selected these herself for you."

"Thank you," I drew my dress over my head and accepted her assistance in getting the new gown on me. The bodice laced in the back, and Luella pulled the strings tight, forcing the air from my lungs. I gazed in the golden mirror propped by the wardrobe. The gown was breathtaking. The neckline plunged daringly to my navel while the fabric clung to every curve, like the way my fighting leathers fit. "Is this too revealing for breakfast?"

Luella fought back a laugh, failing miserably. "This is modest compared to what you'll see at court. Half the ladies here parade themselves before the prince like peacocks, hoping to catch his eye." She paused, studying my expression. "Are you uncomfortable?"

"Well, I don't suppose you'd let me down there in a tunic and leggings?"

"It's not about what I'll allow, Lady Alora. You could wear what you prefer for all I care. But for formal meals and events, the queen expects attire befitting your station. You are to be queen, after all."

"You're quite bold for a lady's maid speaking to the future queen," I said with mock haughtiness, watching her reaction.

A blush crept up her golden neck as she bowed. "I'm sorry, I meant no offense."

"Please, I was only teasing. You're far more pleasant company than our stern friend who brought you here." I smiled at her from the mirror as Luella began to fix my hair. She wove a golden headpiece into my long locks, leaving the rest tumbling down my shoulders in dark curls.

"I try not to be quite so rigid." She surveyed her work and smiled approvingly. "Please don't repeat what you said to her face. She'll make your life hell here."

"Let her try. I prefer your company anyway."

"We should hurry before you're late." She opened my chamber door, gesturing for me to lead. I nearly collided with a wall of armor. Looking up, I met the stern gaze of a guard, his brows drawn together beneath steel-grey hair, a matching mustache framing his firm mouth. "My lady, this is Magnus Thane, your appointed guard. He and I will accompany you from now on."

Magnus Thane bowed deeply, his steely eyes meeting my gaze, "My life and blade are yours, Lady Alora." His expression remained stoic as he straightened, betraying nothing but years of practiced formality.

Magnus followed us quietly as we made our way to the dining hall. With Luella leading the way, I arrived before I was beyond fashionably late. The royal family was seated at the grand table. The king and queen sat at its head with their sons flanking them like golden sentinels. Upon my entry, Oryn and Davian rose. I continued forward, questioning where I should sit. My bond pulsed with an urgent need to go to Ryn, who was taking measured steps towards me, sunlight catching in his golden hair like flames dancing across a morning sky. His presence filled the room like summer heat, and my skin prickled with awareness of every step he took closer.

"Lor, sit with me!" Davian called out eagerly. Ryn's head snapped to his younger brother, muscles tensing like a lion preparing to strike.

"It's her first meal with us and you're already trying to steal my wife from me?" Ryn's voice carried a dangerous edge beneath its playful tone.

"She's not your wife yet," Davian crossed his arms like a petulant child. "Besides, she was my friend first. You hardly know her."

"Hardly know her—" Ryn caught himself before he could say more. A flush crept up his neck. *Ah, Oryn hadn't told his family about our night in the tavern. At least I could mark the story I imagined in the paper about me targeting him out of my growing list of negative possibilities.* "When did you meet her?"

"She's the one who saved me. Her and Raven."

At the sound of his name, I missed the steed. I made a mental note to check on him. Last I heard, he was behaving as much as he could at the town's stables. The old warhorse was a survivor, but knowing him, the stable hands were probably too terrified to complain.

So you're the one I should thank for my brother's safe return. The Fates seem determined to entwine our paths, Love. Ryn's voice slid like honey through our bond. A hint of jealousy marked his tone. Even with his brother's innocence, my mate's possessive nature flared.

"You're the one who found Davian?" The queen's voice cut through the tension.

Ryn's fingers found mine as he led me towards the seat beside him. He pulled my chair out with practiced grace and settled me forward once I was seated. His chair scraped closer to mine as he sat, his thigh brushing against my skirts.

"I did. When I came into town to help my uncle, I stopped at a stream for water and found him in a bush, dirty and half-starved."

"Thank you for bringing him home," the queen said, her voice carrying the practiced warmth of someone who'd mastered the art of royal gratitude. Just as quickly as she'd engaged me in conversation, she returned her attention to the plate before her. Davian slumped in his seat across from me, his bottom lip jutting out in a way that reminded me he was still more boy than prince.

The meal dragged on in uncomfortable silence, broken only by Ryn's persistent attempts at small talk. I answered him with short, clipped answers, counting the moments until escape, resisting both his physical warmth and the pull of our bond. If every meal would be this torturous, I might need to find an excuse to take my meals elsewhere. After more formal exchanges about military strategies between father and son, we were finally excused. As I hurried to the great double doors, fighting against the mating bond's insistent pull, warm fingers encircled my wrist. I turned to find Ryn, his touch sending sparks through my skin, our connection flaring to life like stars in twilight.

"Are you still up for that tour later?" Hope danced in his eyes while my body sang at his touch. I smiled and nodded.

"Can't wait," I said, the words both truth and torment. My heart thundered against my ribs, the thread between us pulling at me like a hook buried deep in my chest, even as every instinct screamed at me to run.

If I couldn't control these feelings, I'd lose more than just my heart—I'd fail everything I came here to do.

CHAPTER 30

After breakfast, Magnus and Luella flank me as we make our way to my next appointment the dreaded afternoon tea with the noble ladies. When Luella had informed me of the engagement after our return to my chambers, I'd contemplated hurling myself from the balcony.

I could track a mark through a blizzard, steal the crown jewels without detection, and end a man's life without hesitation, but an hour of mindless chatter with these noble daughters felt like a special kind of torment.

Considering Luella's warning about their bitter resentment over my engagement to their precious prince, I would rather face a hundred armed guards than endure their false pleasantries.

Who would have thought Death's Wraith would quiver at the thought of a little tea party? Maël's voice echoed through my mind with that familiar mocking lilt.

Thank the gods Oryn couldn't hear Maël's voice in my head.

If he knew I spoke with my dead fiancé while plotting treason, I'd

If you were real, I'd drive my blade between your ribs.

Careful, little hunter. Your threats only excite me more.

A scoff escaped my lips before I could stop it. If Luella heard, she was too well-mannered to comment.

"Do you think Oryn could rescue me from this nightmare?" I ask Luella as we follow my silent sentinel.

Her laugh echoes through the vast hallway, drawing a sharp glance from Magnus.

"If you want your life in the palace to become unbearable, then by all means." Luella pauses before the garden doors where the tea awaits.

"Show any weakness, and they'll descend like vultures. Having Prince Oryn rescue you from a tea party? They'd never let you forget it. The rumors would spread like wildfire, worse than what's already being whispered in dark corners. Remember, respect is a two-way street in this court."

I freeze, my heart stuttering. "Wait. What rumors are already spreading?"

She dismisses my concern with a wave. "Focus on showing these noble daughters that their games mean nothing to you."

She gives me an encouraging smile and a gentle push toward where Magnus stands, door held wide.

I meet his gaze, bracing for the morning's cold reception. But something different glimmers in those grey eyes.

"I don't suppose you'd grant me mercy with that sword of yours?" I glance at Magnus's weapon hopefully. "It would give me a perfect excuse to skip this nightmare."

"My blade serves to protect you, not harm you," Magnus replied, his voice low and firm. "The girl speaks true. Walk in there with your head high, or they'll devour you whole. But should any of them dare to harm you, call for me. I'll come."

His words, though not quite the rescue I'd hoped for, settled something in my chest. I didn't need protection. Gods knew any of these nobles who tried to harm me would find my blade in their heart before they drew their next breath. Still, knowing someone would answer if I called stirred an unfamiliar warmth in my chest as I entered this nest of vipers.

The noble women perched around delicate tables adorned with lace and flowers like perfectly posed dolls. Their endless chatter faltered as I approached the center table where Luella had directed me earlier. The women rose in unison, offering gentle bows as they introduced themselves. Then my gaze caught on a familiar face - the brunette from before, her blonde shadow relegated to a distant table. She introduced herself as Ingrid.

"A pleasure to meet you all," I murmured, matching their bow before claiming my seat at the head of the table. Conversation fluttered to life as servants filled our cups with steaming tea. I doctored mine with cream and sugar, letting the delicate floral notes dance across my tongue.

"You must be thrilled," Elliana gushed from my right, delicately biting into a shortbread cookie. "Prince Oryn is absolutely divine."

"He is," I admitted, cursing the warmth that crept up my neck. "The whole situation feels rather surreal." And it was true - whether I wanted this or not, anyone would find it strange to go from a normal life to suddenly being engaged to a prince. Especially one so highly revered.

Ingrid's scoff cut through the pleasant atmosphere like a blade, her teacup barely concealing her sneer. The other women tensed, their expressions shifting from placid to wary. "I'm sure you're not complaining about your fairy tale ending. Though I wonder if your uncle has found someone to replace you yet. Such a pity you came to help him only to abandon him so quickly."

I set my cup down and meet her cold, narrowed gaze. "It is a shame, I truly loved my time at the book shop. He won't have a need for me after I find a suitable replacement to help my dear uncle." I pick up one of the dainty cookies and take a small bite before setting it down. "These are just so lovely." I muse.

The ladies murmur their agreement as they sample the delicate pastries. Ingrid's gaze remains fixed on me, unyielding with hate.

"Don't mind her," Elliana leans close to whisper, glancing nervously at the other girls like prey watching for predators. "I heard her parents were negotiating a betrothal between her and the prince before the king began fixating on the prophecy." Most of the ladies wore calm masks as they chatted and sipped their tea, but some, like Ingrid, looked ready to turn this frivolous occasion into a blood bath.

"How curious that you appear in town and suddenly find yourself chosen," Ingrid's voice dripped with venom. "Surely there are ladies here of far more...distinguished lineage than a mere shopkeeper's niece."

"The Fates work in mysterious ways," I replied, keeping my voice light. "I never wanted to take that assessment. A prince marrying someone like me? The very idea is laughable."

A laugh escaped my lips as the women's eyes darted between us like frightened birds.

"And yet, here we sit." Ingrid's sour expression had my fingers twitching, yearning for the familiar comfort of my dagger. How lovely that blade would look buried in her pale throat.

Her judgment meant nothing. I knew what I was - an assassin playing at being a princess, soon to be queen. The absurdity of it all burned in my chest. I never asked for any of this.

Her endless lecture about bloodlines faded to meaningless noise. Every sip of the floral tea felt like an eternity, a waste of time when I could be gaining the intell I desperately needed.

When I noticed the other tables emptying, I seized my chance. Rising with practiced grace, I offered the ladies a farewell before gliding from the room.

Relief flooded through me at the sight of Magnus's perpetually grumpy expression. He looked as thrilled about waiting through this ridiculous affair as I felt.

"Did the tea party meet your expectations, Lady Alora?" Magnus asked, his expression caught between amusement and concern.

"I'd rather face down an army," I admitted, checking that neither Luella nor Miss Gregoria lurked nearby to witness my breach of etiquette. "Could we visit the garden? I need to breathe air that isn't perfumed with false pleasantries."

"Of course," Magnus said, guiding us through a door into the lush rose garden.

"So you prefer war over tea?" His deep chuckle resonated in the garden. "That's certainly a first."

If only he knew who he was speaking to. Maël's laughter echoed in my mind before fading like morning mist, there and gone on his own wild whims.

My expression must have betrayed something because Magnus's laughter grew when our eyes met.

"Give me steel and blood over false smiles any day," I said.

"Strange. I'd expect Augustus's niece to excel at mind games. Your uncle always had a razor-sharp wit about him."

I settled onto a stone bench, patting the space beside me. Magnus shook his head, assuming his guard position at my side like a stalwart shadow.

"I had no idea you knew my uncle," I said, anxiety coiling in my gut. The old man never mentioned knowing anyone inside the castle, I kept my face calm, inconspicuously checking my options of an exit. If my cover was already blown, I'd have to find my way to Johan some other way.

"I was stationed in Bridgedale years ago when he lived there with your aunt," Magnus said, his voice warm with memories. "I must admit, I was shocked when you appeared. Vanya always seemed too wild to settle into motherhood."

I could picture them crossing paths in some dimly lit tavern, Vanya expertly relieving him of his coin through bets he'd lost before he even made them. My master had always excelled at reading people, turning simple card games into elaborate mental traps.

"I was adopted," I said carefully, watching his reaction. "I never knew my parents."

The silence from my weekly letters to Vanya burned like acid in my chest, but I made a mental note to ask about Magnus in my next one.

"My father served as a soldier there," I said, crafting the lie with practiced ease. "And my mother... well, she was flighty. I've been told I am her mirrored image." The half-truth felt bitter on my tongue, but I prayed it would satisfy his curiosity.

Magnus's face softened with sympathy as he murmured platitudes about perhaps crossing paths with my father.

Like everyone else, he probably assumed my father met his end on the front lines, becoming another nameless soldier ground to ash between the warring kingdoms.

We resumed our stroll and he steered our conversation back to the tea gathering. I recounted Ingrid's barely veiled insults about my inexperience with court life.

"There's more to ruling than having the right bloodline," he said, his voice hard with conviction. "Sounds to me like she's nothing but a jealous harlot."

A laugh bubbled up as I imagined Ingrid's horrified face at the insult. I hadn't expected this gruff warrior to lift my spirits after the morning's disaster. Usually, he was granite and steel. Untouchable. Coiled tension ready to strike. Much like my Raven - both of them forged for battle, not these delicate social games. I didn't realize I'd spoken that last part aloud until Magnus responded.

"I remind you of a raven?" he asked, brows furrowing.

"No," I said, shaking my head. "You remind me of my horse,

Raven. You have similar mannerisms." The words tumbled out before I could stop them.

"You're saying I act like a horse?" His voice held a dangerous edge.

I winced, scrambling to salvage the situation. "Please forget I said anything, you do not act like a horse. He acts like you."

After a few quiet steps, Magnus's voice cut through the silence. "Wait, is this the demon horse the city stable has been talking about?"

"He's not a demon," I protested, heat rising to my cheeks. "He's just selective about his company."

His eyes narrowed to dangerous slits, "One of my men almost came back with a few less fingers after he was called to help wrangle the bastard."

"Well, he shouldn't have touched him without permission," I said with a defiant lift of my chin. "Like I said, he's very particular. Davian and I have no issue approaching him."

He shook his head, muttering something that sounded like a prayer for patience. Pride swelled in my chest as I smiled, pleased that Raven kept his wild spirit. Domestication be damned, he was born for battlefields and glory, for making grown men tremble in their boots.

"I'll add you to his list of approved attendees," I teased, enjoying the way his face paled slightly.

"I choose life," he said dryly, though the corner of his mouth twitched.

THE LIBRARY DOORS creaked as Luella and I slipped inside, seeking refuge from the earlier drama of the queen's tea. Books stretched endlessly from floor to ceiling, their weathered spines glinting with gold and forgotten promises. The scent of aged paper and ink wrapped around us like a familiar embrace. I felt a familiar pang in my chest, remembering the cozy bookshop nestled in the heart of the capital.

"I spend most of my free time here," Luella confessed, running her fingers along the shelves. "The other handmaidens think I'm odd."

"Then we can be odd together." I followed her deeper into the stacks. Books had been my sanctuary since childhood, though my grandmother's collection paled in comparison to this. A familiar ache bloomed in my chest as memories of countless nights spent curled up with her books washed over me, each one a treasured escape from the weight of simply existing.

Luella pulled out a massive tome bound in midnight blue leather. "This one's my favorite - Ancient Prophecies and Portents." She set it on a nearby table, dust motes dancing in the sunbeams streaming through tall windows.

"The stories of the lost gods always intrigued me, I like to think I would've been one of their acolytes in another life." She looked down at the heavy tome with a distant smile, one I knew well. I understood that dreamy expression. How many times had I lost myself in imagined lives, in countless adventures waiting to unfold?

As she flipped through yellowed pages, I caught glimpses of intricate illustrations - constellations, mythical creatures, and elaborate symbols. She stopped at a page marked with a silk ribbon.

"This prophecy has been discussed more lately," she said, pointing to flowing script.

"Several claim it foretells the victor between realms." The ancient words danced before my eyes like living things, an ethereal glow seeming to pulse beneath the ink as candlelight caught each carefully penned letter.

When shadows lengthen and stars align, the weaver of fate will tie the strings.

Powers once separated shall intertwine, unleashing power to shatter the world's very bones.

The harbinger of flame and fate will save us all, a beacon in the darkness a blade of all. Those who dare to wield this power will rise, crowned in formidable glory.

In the forge of blazing fate and destiny's weave, a power beyond reckoning will awaken and cleave. For the merging of might that dances just beyond, a siren's call of glory and bonds unbound.

My breath caught as I read the prophetic text a second time. The words resonated in my bones like a forgotten melody. But that was absurd. Prophecies were nothing more than the wine-soaked ramblings of long-dead mystics... weren't they?

"What do you make of it?" Luella asked.

I forced a casual shrug, grateful she couldn't see my trembling hands. "Just another prophet trying their hand at poetry. Though I'll give them credit for their dramatic flair."

Luella's laughter danced between the shelves, a warm ring in the dust-filled air. The scent of aged leather bindings mingled with the musty sweetness of forgotten pages, while golden afternoon light caught the dancing motes like falling stars.

"The king believes you're the key to ending this war. That's why he wants Prince Oryn to marry you. He sees something in you, a power that could finally bring our people peace."

I let her words settle in the space between us.

"I'm no one special," I said, the lie burning my tongue. "I don't have any power that could end a war."

"The mage disagrees. Come on," she set the tome down, then ushered me out of the library with haste. "Your castle tour awaits."

I followed her quietly, her earlier words ringing in my head. Though shadows coursed through my veins like liquid night, I couldn't believe they'd turn the tides of war. What could darkness offer except more destruction?

Sweet, naive Luella, holding fast to dreams of peace while the king's appetite for power twisted like a serpent in the dark. Her people's salvation would mean another's destruction.

The prophecy's mention of shadows and flame sent a chill of recognition across my skin, but I shoved that truth into the darkest corners of my mind, focusing instead on fortifying the walls around my heart before facing my mate again.

CHAPTER 31

Ryn's tour of my new home was surprisingly anticlimactic. Though I'd worried over resisting the magnetic pull between us, he kept his word, never pushing beyond the boundaries I set for us. He let me set the pace without a single complaint. When I permitted him to hold my hand, it seemed to quiet the insistent tug of the thread between us, though my body hummed with an aching need for more.

Day after day, I spent time with Ryn, who—much to my chagrin—discovered my complete lack of directional sense. If my perpetual confusion frustrated him, his patient smile never wavered as he guided me through the same corridors until he was reasonably sure I wouldn't lose my way. When I wasn't with Oryn, I was either being paraded around by the king and queen like their prized pet, or finding refuge in Luella's companionship.

Each morning, Ryn escorted us to the library, a ritual I found myself cherishing despite myself. He insisted it was to give Magnus a break, though I knew full well he had arranged for someone else to take the night watch.

The prince had found his loophole—satisfying our bond through these careful moments of proximity. Each second without him became an eternity, and I found myself counting breaths until our next meeting, even as I fought against the longing. The mate bond thrummed beneath my skin like a living thing, each moment of resistance leaving me physically drained and emotionally raw.

At night I snuck out of my room, finding it easier without Magnus' hawk-like senses. In the quiet dark, I skulked around the castle. All traces of Johan had vanished since that day in the throne room. Moving around undetected became easier after I snuck out to the bookshop to retrieve my knives, leathers, and boots. The cool leather against my skin and the familiar weight of my blades at my hips felt like coming home.

I sent what information I could to Vanya, but it seemed standard for a king trying to expand his territory. Army movements here, terrible assassination ideas there. None of which seemed to yield the desired result. Sunneva continued decimating towns on the edge of Esmeray, leaving no room for doubt on how powerful the Sunnevan army was. The king, however, seemed on edge, erupting at a moment's notice at Davian's jokes or lecturing Oryn about seizing his destiny. His eyes, once steady and calculating, now darted about the room as if searching for unseen threats. His fingers drummed incessantly on the arm of his throne, a constant staccato of unease.

Today, Ryn came to fetch me before lunch, a wild grin on his face. "My lady," he held out a hand for me as I stepped through my doorway. "I was hoping you'd be up for a little adventure today."

"A prince after my own heart," I mused. "Do we have time for an adventure when the ball is tonight?"

"I promise we'll be back in time." Ryn led us out of the castle grounds to the stable within the main walls. A young man brought a tall white horse out to Oryn, who accepted it with a smile. He steadied his steed as I climbed into the saddle. He slid in behind me, his muscular thighs pressing against mine. We rode as if being chased, and I couldn't help but smile and laugh with glee as he guided us through the town streets towards the city gates. The wind whipped through my dark hair, making me long for my own handsome steed. Though the updates from the stable were positive, I still worried and longed to ride him. Miss Gregoria packed my schedule day after day, leaving me barely able to continue my correspondence with Vanya. Sending useful information without being obvious had become increasingly difficult, and I had no doubt the head of household scrutinized all my letters. The walls of the palace now felt like a gilded cage, suffocating my freedom and purpose.

As we neared the main gates, Ryn steered us left, heading towards the stables. There, Raven stood tall, his eyes locked on me, hooves stomping the hard ground. Dust swirled around him and the poor stable hand struggling to maintain his calm and hold onto the reins.

"Raven!" Waiting for Oryn to dismount felt like torture. I didn't miss the feel of his hands on my waist as I swung my leg over the saddle and jumped to the ground. His horse was large, but Raven towered over it like a king. I threw my arms around the warhorse, cooing over his handsomeness and how much I'd missed him. He didn't seem to have the heart to punish me, nuzzling me with his nose and sniffing my pockets for treats. In that moment, I felt awful. I'd always brought him treats. Had I known I'd see him today, I would've brought a stash.

Oryn cleared his throat and nudged my arm behind me, placing some treats in my hands. I beamed at him.

"Thank you." I could almost feel my eyes watering as I turned back to hold my offerings out to Raven, who took them greedily.

"I've been curious about him ever since Davian mentioned him." Ryn gave his own horse a handful of food before coming to greet Raven. The warhorse eyed him warily, sizing him up with his head held high. After a few beats, he let out a snort and pushed at the prince's pocket where the treats had originated. "I think he likes me."

Ryn laughed as Raven accepted a treat from his hand. He patted the steed's neck, looking over his expansive back.

"Hard not to when you bring such yummy treats." I couldn't keep my eyes off my horse. "I've missed you," I said to him, receiving a low whinny in response. I looked over to Oryn. "Do we have time for a ride?"

"I was hoping you'd say that." He summoned the stable hand to fetch my saddle. "I thought it might be good to bring him home with us. That way, you can see him every day and be able to ride him more. And if Miss Gregoria has you too busy, Davian or I can sneak out and feed him treats on your behalf."

He flashed me that gorgeous smile of his, and I lit up with happiness. I threw my arms around his neck, his arms sliding around my waist to press me against him. Before I could think better of it, I planted my lips on his. What started as more of a peck turned into him claiming my mouth. His hand came up to twist into my hair, deepening our kiss.

"I'll do whatever I can to make you smile like you just did, Lor. No matter what, you are more than duty to me. You are everything."

I kissed him again, unable to resist. I allowed myself to enjoy this moment, this wonderfully happy moment, at least until reality came crashing down. Because I would find Johan, and I would kill him. When Oryn realized what I'd done, I was sure he'd wish he'd never crossed paths with me.

You don't understand what a man in love will do, Alora. Not everything is so black and white.

Goody, mind Maël was in one of his know-it-all moods. *Most people are not so accepting of my occupation. I wouldn't be surprised if I was on a wanted list here.*

Oh, you most definitely are, he let out a short laugh, *but that doesn't mean he'd be so quick to send you to the dungeon. Take it from someone who knows, you're a hard girl to walk away from.* His voice softened, a hint of longing creeping in. *Trust me, Lor. I've tried.*

It's no surprise Raven and I left Oryn and his horse in the dust as we took off for a friendly race. By the time he matched our pace, he was grumbling about cheating. I didn't tell him Raven's origins. I just laughed and said my mount must've had some pent up energy to burn off.

Oryn escorted me back to my rooms, leaving me to prepare for our ball. Never in my life did I imagine attending my own ball, being paraded as the king's prized future daughter-in-law. Though Oryn might see me as a person, the king saw only his ticket to victory, a weapon to wield. He didn't even know what that power truly meant.

The image of the blindingly white flames flashed across my mind. I imagined them licking up the very walls of this golden palace. Could they obliterate it like they did the cottages? Would the castle still crumble to ash? Somehow, I knew nothing in this realm could withstand my fire. A shiver ran its way down my spine as I recalled the experience. My question would go unanswered. Never again would I dare call upon that power. I'll stick to my shadows—at least there, I know what lurks in the dark.

A knock sounded at the door made me turn when Magnus held it open for a delighted Luella, who skipped in, another gorgeous gown in her arms. "We need to get you ready, Prince Oryn will be here any minute to escort you." She was more excited than I was for the ball.

"Will you be attending?" I let her help me slide the gorgeous, silky fabric over my head. She led me to the vanity to paint my face and sort my dark hair into something presentable.

"And risk the wrath of Miss Gregoria? I'll have to live vicariously through your stories later and what I happen to see as I'm ordered around."

"How about we trade places? I can hide in here and you can

pretend to be me and dance the night away." I chuckled, knowing I would happily stay in my room.

"I think Prince Oryn would notice you weren't you." She shook her head at me as she took a comb to my hair, coaxing it into waves that fell down my shoulders. The pieces near my face she braided into a crown that curled on top of my head. Little glittering gems were added between the plaits. "Besides, all eyes will be on you tonight. It will be wonderful!" She beamed as she assessed her work.

The thought of all those eyes on me made my stomach churn.

During our return, Oryn spoke of his closest friend's impending return. His longest companion, who'd fought alongside him during his father's missions. Apparently, this was the friend he had met when I thought he'd abandoned me at the tavern. Oryn explained his friend hadn't been celebrating the night prior—he'd been investigating something.

A flutter of anxiety rippled through my chest. Not only would I have to face the entire court tonight, but now I'd have to meet Oryn's dearest friend. Someone whose opinion of me would matter deeply to my mate, whether I wanted it to or not.

I glanced at myself in the mirror, unable to recognize the woman before me. Luella had dressed me in a silver dress, so light it was almost white. Two glittering straps held it up and plunged down my back, not meeting the remainder of the fabric until just above my rear. The silk felt cool on my skin, showing a hint of my peaked nipples. Luella had gone a bit dramatic with my makeup, dark kohl lined my violet eyes, making the strange color stand out. My cheeks held a hint of pink in just the right spots and my lips were painted a sultry red.

"You're an artist," I murmured, my hand barely grazing my cheek as I stared in wonder.

"Oh, hush," Luella chided. A knock at the door alerted us it was time. Luella rushed to the door with a squeak and opened it, revealing my handsome mate on the other side. He was dressed in a black coat, adorned with a shiny sun pin. A golden crown rested upon his unbound blonde hair. His eyes traveled from the ground to my face, drinking me in.

He gazed at me as though he loved me, and it made my heart both soar and shatter, each beat a war between hope and harsh reality. I had to remind myself the only reason I was in this situation was because his father thought our marriage will bring him a victory in this dreadful war. Did Oryn view this the same? Our mate bond was happenstance, something that wasn't accounted for and wouldn't have mattered. Our union was the key.

He seemed to find his words as he walked to me, his hands grazing my bare arms. "You look amazing." He placed a kiss on my cheek, then traveled behind my ear, humming as he trailed his nose along my neck. The intimacy of his breath on my skin peppered me with goosebumps. "Ready?" His eyes found mine as he held out a hand to me. I placed mine in his awaiting palm and smiled.

"Please don't leave my side tonight," I begged as we left my rooms and headed down the hallway.

"I wouldn't dream of it, Love," he assured me. Magnus trailed behind us quietly. *I was hoping you'd want to stay by my side after the ball as well.*

You mean stay the night?

He nodded at my perplexed look. *Only if you want. You're under no obligation to do so, Lor. I won't force you.*

I would very much like to spend the night with him again if it was like the tavern. Every moment we had spent I had found myself wishing for his touch all over my body, my body demanding to writhe beneath him.

I'll consider it. I gave him a sly smile and squeezed his arm with my hand reassuringly.

He grinned, eyeing me all over again. I suppressed a groan at how he was undressing me with his eyes. This dress would likely not last the night.

Upon reaching the ballroom, we were announced by name and cheers erupted. Oryn and I led the first dance, and I was surprised by how much I was enjoying twirling in his arms. We enjoyed a few more songs before we joined his family at the head table set up on the dais. Beside Oryn's smaller throne, another seat was placed for me. I was thankful he was a buffer between the king and me. The king had not held back his glee for the match and excitement for the prophecy to come to pass upon our wedding day, his calculating eyes gleaming with barely concealed triumph as he watched us. I caught Oryn roll his eyes at his father's words.

Everyone found a seat at the surrounding tables and the grand feast began. Davian came over to me, insisting I try all of his favorites. His older brother tried to shoo him away but the young man dismissed the attempts, telling him I was his friend first. Oryn grumbled his annoyances as he continued to eat, the corner of his mouth lifting up in amusement. Davian finally left me to the rest of my food after I told him each item he'd chosen was absolutely delicious. I could hear him relay his triumph to his mother at the other end of the table, pride swelling in his chest. The Queen always had so few words to share, but her ears belonged to her youngest son.

This constant battle over your attention is getting a bit tiring, just tell Davian I'm your favorite, Oryn chuckled in my mind as I tried not to spit my food out.

Who said you're my favorite?

A deep growl rumbled down the bond. *It sure seemed like I was when my tongue was between those delicious thighs.*

The room suddenly felt warm, my thoughts flashing back to the night we spent together. Oblivious at the time of our bond that had solidified. The way he kissed me, touched me, a never-ending montage of heat.

You're ridiculous for being in a competition with him. He's your little brother.

And yet, I still feel jealous when he's trying to sit beside you or has your attention. My place is at your side.

I thought it was my place by your side. A quiet little wife for the prince to sit pretty upon the throne.

I'm not that kind of male, Lor, though I was only teasing, his voice was stern, *we'd be equals, rule side by side. And I much prefer you not be quiet. Especially when you start making those delightful little noises...*

I'm starting to think this bond is cursing you with lunacy.

If it is, I'll gladly live the rest of my life cursed under your enthrall. I can't help but be obsessed with you.

Oryn set his fork down as a tall, dark-haired fae male approached. The male wore a formal black tunic that melded with his dark leather pants.

"Kyler!" Oryn leapt from his seat with a grin, meeting him at the steps.

They clasped arms, and I took in the newcomer's presence. A sword hung at his hip, completing his dark ensemble.

"I hope I'm not too late," his deep voice reached me, stirring an inexplicable sense of familiarity. He sounded like I'd imagined every male lead in my favorite books. That must be it. I studied him, searching my memory for any previous encounter. Surely I would remember him if I had. Across the room, I caught Ingrid's cold gaze. Her eyes flicked between Oryn and Kyler then narrowed again as she met my stare.

Oryn guided him behind the table, and I rose to greet them.

"Kyler, meet Alora, my future queen." Gods, Oryn's voice swelled with such pride, as though I were his long-awaited salvation rather than his father's prophesied tool.

"It's nice to meet you, Lady Alora." Kyler bowed, and I answered with a graceful curtsy.

"A pleasure." As our eyes met, something snapped taut within me like a bowstring drawn too tight. His deep brown eyes widened as if he felt it too. The wine from my private drinking game—taking a sip every time the king mentioned the prophecy - was hitting harder than expected. I fought to keep my balance, determined not to appear like some swooning court lady.

"The pleasure's all mine," Kyler's voice cut through the haze like a blade. The boys fell into conversation, and heat crept up my neck.

"Excuse me," I murmured, though Oryn was deep in conversation with Kyler. His attention snapped to me instantly, his arm snaking around my waist.

"Are you okay?" He whispered against my ear.

I waved him off like swatting away a persistent fly. "Just need a little fresh air. I don't want to pull you away from your friend. I'll be back, I promise."

He nodded at Magnus, who stood vigilant near the dais. "Don't stray too far, Love." His grip loosened, and I felt his gaze follow me as I carefully descended the dais and slipped through the balcony doors. The night air hit my face, and clarity slowly returned.

"Everything alright, my lady?" Magnus stepped just behind me, his face etched with concern.

"I'm fine, it was just suffocating in there." I moved to the railing, pressing my palms against the cool marble. Below, the gardens sprawled out in moonlit splendor. Voices drifted up from below, drawing my attention. Two figures stood in conference—one I recognized as the king, whose absence from the ball I'd barely noticed, too busy drinking through his prophecy speeches. The other lurked in shadow, features obscured.

"Just get it done." The king's command cut through the night before he stalked away, likely heading back before his absence was noted.

His conspirator emerged from the shadows, making his way through the garden. As he turned, his profile caught the moonlight, and my world tilted on its axis like a ship in a storm. The king's secret meeting wasn't with just anyone—it was with Johan. The implications of this discovery sent ice through my veins.

CHAPTER 32

Without wasting another breath, I whirled back toward the celebration.

Oryn and Kyler still chatted near the head table, while the revelers had succumbed to raucous merriment. The room echoed with laughter as fae and mortals alike spun to the music, their tankards of ale and wine sloshing dangerously.

I set my sights on a hallway just to the right of the balcony area. It would be the fastest way out of here. Keeping to the shadows, I slipped past, praying my betrothed wouldn't spot me.

With each step, the cacophony of the party faded. Once I no longer could hear the music, I looked around and confirmed I'm finally alone. I brought shadows around me, covering me in darkness. Now cloaked, I ran towards the first set of stairs and continued towards the gardens. Mercifully, this part of the castle was home to straightforward passages.

My heart sank as I realized all traces of Johan had vanished, as if the wind itself had conspired to erase his existence in the brief time it took me to reach the lush gardens. I couldn't find so much as a boot print. I rushed through the main paths and checked each exit

After about twenty minutes, I had accepted he's gone without a trace. That murderous bastard was probably sleeping soundly by now, his conscience soothed by the blood money he earned from our so-called rulers.

I made my way back to the ballroom where the music had shifted to a sweet melody. Just before entering, I disbanded my shadows, the loss of them sending a shiver down my spine. I felt naked, especially in the revealing dress chosen for me. I surveyed the party, no one appeared to notice my absence. I'd feared my new status would draw unwanted attention, complicating my efforts to investigate. But the royal fae were truly wrapped up in themselves, appointing a nobody like me as the future princess was good for a laugh but not enough to halt their interests in their own quest for gaining more power in their social standing.

I returned to the dais, finding Kyler gone and in his place, a nobleman from a neighboring town speaking in hushed tones with Oryn. The male didn't see me approach from his right, but Ryn's blue eyes tracked my every step.

"...You should be marrying my Tatiana, sire. She's of noble breed, very powerful in fire magic. She would be honored to give you an heir worthy of the crown." The nobleman slurred. Ryn's gaze turned razor sharp as he seized the man's throat, lifting him until his boots barely scraped the stone floor.

"Lord Yrenez, I don't believe I asked for your choice of my wife when I asked you how the pumpkin crop was this season. I most certainly did not ask for the hand of your wretched daughter," he growled. The crowd before us hushed, the music even quieter than before. "Lady Alora was deemed chosen by the gods themselves, in more ways than one the most powerful match for me. Do you dare defy the gods."

Lord Yrenez whimpered and violently tried to shake his head. "No, sire, I misspoke—"

"If you ever speak of Lady Alora again, or bring up your wretch of an offspring, you will find yourself at the wrong end of my sword." Oryn let Yrenez go, the older male crumbling to the ground, holding a hand to his own throat and struggling to stumble away. His hunched over body disappeared into the crowd. Ryn faced the attendees, all in a trance of shock, "For anyone else who believes the gods are wrong, they are not. Lady Alora is my gods given mate." Soft cries of shock rumbled through the crowd. "She is the only one my heart and my throne will ever belong to. Anyone who turns a sharp tongue or blade against her is considered to have made that statement about the crown itself and will be punished, severely." His stare was like a shard of ice as he looked deep into the nervous souls of his gathered people. Some seemed to shift their stance, many looked down to the floor, very few were bold enough to meet his unyielding gaze.

His ferocity sent a thrill through me, and I found myself following that dull buzz, that golden thread humming between us, drawing me to his side. My hand found its way to his chest, almost of its own accord. It's like he finally took a breath and began to relax under my touch, his arm wrapping around me protectively.

The king rose from his throne and cleared his throat. "We are honored to have such a blessed union tomorrow." He raised his almost overflowing goblet of wine towards us. "To the future of Sunneva."

"Sun blessed," the crowd answered.

Oryn leaned by my ear, the warmth of his breath tickling the side of my face. "Ready to get out of here, Love?"

I nodded, letting him take his hand in mine and lead us out of the throng of drunken fae. My gaze swept the crowd, cataloging potential threats. It's clear many of them would rather see a blade in my heart than a crown on my head. A shiver ran down my spine as I caught several pairs of eyes glaring daggers at my back.

CHAPTER 33

The crown prince's chambers were more opulent than mine. As expected for the heir to the throne. Warm wooden floors flowed throughout the suite, with an intimate sitting area near the entrance. Two chairs and a sofa the color of summer skies sat before a stone fireplace. A wooden archway led to his bedchamber.

"Wine, Love?" he asked as I mapped the quarters in my mind. Two exits—the door we entered and the balcony doors near his four-poster bed. A resplendent golden sun spread across his ceiling.

"I'd love some." Instead of taking one of the azure chairs, I explored his room, where he didn't have gold accents, he had that same blue. The decorator had clearly favored a theme. I stopped at a large oak desk, adorned with another sun motif. Parchment lay in neat piles near a quill. I perched upon its edge as he approached with the promised beverage. He seemed distracted, his mind anywhere but here with me. It hurt a bit; despite my plans to leave, I had glowed internally in the ballroom. This male had denounced any possibility of wanting another. He had chosen me above all when every single one of those nobles thought I wasn't worthy. They knew

I wasn't worthy. The irony stung—their disdain only matched by my own self-doubt, even as their prince claimed me as his.

Oryn sighed as he placed his hands on either side of my thighs on the hard desk and placed his head on my shoulder. I brushed a loose strand of his golden mane off his face, releasing a subtle citrus scent into the air, mingling with the warmth of his skin and the lingering spice of wine on his breath.

"Where are you right now?"

He lifted his head, raking his fingers through his hair. "Those nobles are ruthless. We need to increase your security detail." Magnus and the soldier rotations might not be enough to dissuade them from making an attempt on your life." His finger gently traced my jawline, lifting my eyes up to his. "I'm sorry they marred our engagement party with their pettiness. No woman, fae or human, could ever compare to you. I'd rather give up my throne, my crown, my life than spend it without you, my mate." His voice trembled with raw emotion, his eyes blazing with fierce devotion as he pressed his forehead to mine, his breath mingling with my own.

His words shattered my resolve, my plans of escape dissolving like frost in sunlight. My fingers traced the lines of his sun tattoo, warming beneath my touch.

"I'm not so sure you know who you're chaining yourself to."

His light eyes darkened to stormy seas, desire eclipsing the blue.

"I'm certain you have no idea how sure of this, of you, I am. There'll never be anyone else. Only you."

I silenced him with my lips, and his response was instant. A growl rumbled through his chest.

His hands gripped my waist, lifting me fully onto the desk. Papers scattered to the floor as he stepped between my legs. Our bond flared, desire scorching through my veins. I fisted my hands in his tunic, dragging him down. Our lips met with savage hunger. His hands roamed my body, leaving trails of fire in their wake. I arched into his touch, wrapping my legs around his waist.

His lips blazed a path down my neck. "Gods, I've missed you."

"Then show me." My breathless lips crash upon his once more, desperate for the contact.

He swept me off the desk in one powerful motion. Cool stone pressed against my back as his burning body pinned me to the wall. The intoxicating blend of citrus and sandalwood flooded my senses. Our bond hummed with electricity as his hands traced invisible paths along my body. Not an inch of my skin remained untouched by him.

"Mine," he breathed against my skin. "My mate. My queen."

"Yours," I gasped as his teeth scraped my neck. "Always yours."

His lips found mine again, softer this time but no less passionate. I felt his hard length pressed against my entrance, sliding through my slick heat.

Desperate moans escaped me as I shifted my hips, begging to feel him fill me completely. A dark chuckle rumbled from deep in his chest as his hand wrapped around my throat. He pulled me from the wall and laid me back upon his desk. My thighs spread for him as his hips pinned me to the hard surface. He held me there, captive under his burning gaze while he continued his sweet torture.

"Ryn," I breathed.

His knowing smirk sent fire racing through my veins. Gods, this male would be my undoing. His golden hair caught the firelight like a halo, his muscles rippling beneath sun kissed skin. The deep V of his hips was a temptation made flesh.

"Tell me what you want, Love."

A whine tore from my throat as his touch coiled the tension in my core even tighter.

I want to hear you say it, Love. I want to hear that pretty little mouth beg for the filthy things I want to do to you.

"Oryn, please," I begged. He positioned himself at my entrance but didn't push in even an inch. "I want you, Ryn."

He drove himself into me. We moved together like waves

meeting the shore, inevitable and perfect. The rest of the world fell away until there was nothing but us, our hearts beating in sync, our souls intertwined. Our mate bond pulsed with each thrust, a golden thread of light binding us together as pleasure crested and broke over us both.

Sweat cooled on our skin as we lay tangled in his sheets, my head resting on his chest. His heartbeat thundered beneath my ear, gradually slowing to match mine. The bond between us hummed contentedly, warmth radiating through every fiber of my being, like liquid sunlight flowing through our veins, binding our souls in an eternal dance.

His fingers danced across my bare shoulder, tracing ancient runes only he knew. "Do you remember that night at the tavern?"

"Mmm." I pressed a smile into his warm skin.

"I knew the moment I saw you. My soul recognized my mate when our eyes locked." His chest rose with a deep breath. "When you left the next morning... gods, I thought I'd go mad. I searched every corner of that city for days searched the city like a man possessed. Even royal duties couldn't tear me away until my father threatened to send the entire army."

Guilt burned like acid in my veins. I'd inflicted that wound. Just as I'd planned to do again.

"While I was angry you had left, I prayed to the gods I would find you again. Seeing you in the throne room was nothing less than the answer to every prayer I'd whispered into darkness." His voice dropped to a whisper. "I see our future so clearly, our children running through these halls, their laughter echoing off these walls their footsteps a melody against marble. You and me, building something real here, something eternal."

My heart stuttered in my chest. The picture he painted was everything I'd never dared to want.

"I love you, Alora. More than the crown, more than my own life." He pressed a kiss to my hair. "You're everything."

His words pierced through every defense I'd built. All my carefully constructed plans crumbled to dust. The mere thought of leaving, of existing without his touch, his smile, his love, felt like trying to live without air. The mate bond surged between us, liquid gold threading through my veins, wrapping around my heart like a promise. My skin hummed where it pressed against his, every point of contact a reminder of what I'd be leaving behind. The thought alone made my chest constrict, made the shadows in my mind rear up in protest.

I lifted my head to look at him, drinking in the sight of him like a woman dying of thirst. His eyes were already closed, breath evening out as sleep claimed him.

"I love you too," I whispered, knowing now that I'd stay. Not for the crown he wore or the kingdom he'd rule, but for the heart that beat in time with mine.

CHAPTER 34

I woke to sunlight streaming through the windows, my heart racing with a mix of excitement and nerves. The bed beside me lay empty. Following the ancient tradition that kept grooms from their brides until the ceremony. The vacant sheets stirred memories of that first night with Oryn, when everything felt possible before it all fell apart. We'd been through this before, the first night fate placed us in each other's path, but I pushed away the foreboding feeling, my stomach twisting into knots that threatened to choke me. That night had been different. We'd grown since then, learned to trust each other. Despite the royal family's devotion to tradition, I longed to wake to his radiant smile one last time, even as guilt gnawed at me for wanting what I couldn't keep forever.

The crisp sheets beneath my fingers still held the faintest trace of his scent—citrus and sandalwood—a reminder of what awaited me at the end of this long day. The emptiness of the massive royal chamber seemed to mock me, every shadow harboring memories of nights spent wrapped in his arms, his fingers trailing fire across my skin, his breath hot against my neck as we moved as one beneath these very sheets.

The heavy door creaked open, and swift footsteps approached the bed. Fresh linens and morning dew perfumed the air, intertwining with the remnants of his lingering fragrance. My breath hitched, heart stumbling over itself as the scents mingled, past and present colliding in a dizzying whirl.

I traced the embroidered edge of the sheet, remembering how differently I'd imagined my future would unfold. The weight of tradition pressed down on me like a velvet cage, beautiful but confining. Part of me yearned to slip into the shadows, to chase after the vengeance that still burned in my heart. But another part, the part that had grown and changed since meeting Oryn, whispered that perhaps this was its own kind of strength—choosing love over revenge, choosing to build something new instead of destroying what was broken.

My fingers curled into the sheets, mind warring between the comfort of Oryn's love and the familiar call of darkness. This was the path I'd chosen, yet my soul still trembled with the weight of it all, analyzing every possibility, every consequence, until my thoughts spiraled like autumn leaves in a storm.

Luella's face was bright with joy. "My lady! Today's the day!" she exclaimed, peeling off the covers. She ushered me into the bathroom. A warm bath awaited, citrus-scented oils perfuming the steamy air, their invigorating aroma chasing away the last vestiges of sleep while promising to make my skin glow like moonlit pearls.

"Luella," I reminded her gently. "When it's just us, call me Lor or Alora." It hurt my heart to see how many of the staff were treated by the nobles, and Luella had become my ally here in this sun blessed prison. In the months since my arrival, she'd become more than just a handmaiden, she was my confidante, my anchor in this gilded cage of courtly life.

"Oh, the palace!" Luella gushed. "I've never seen such decorations in all my life. Even the old servants say the king hasn't celebrated this grandly since his wedding to her majesty."

I let Luella's excited chatter wash over me as she helped me bathe, her words blending together in my anxious mind. The warm water should have been soothing, but it did little to calm the storm of thoughts swirling inside me. Each gentle splash against my skin echoed the beating of my uncertain heart, torn between duty and desire, between what was right and what felt inevitable.

"The flowers, my lady," Luella continued, her voice dreamy. "Roses from every corner of the kingdom, and lilies that gleam like they've been blessed by the moon herself."

My head bobbed without thought, my stomach coiling tight.

Wasn't this meant to be the happiest day of my life?

It will be, Maël's voice washed over me like cool water against the brewing storm in my mind.

I squeezed my eyes shut, willing Maël's voice away. During my entire stay in this castle, Johan remained beyond my reach.

A princess who killed would rot in a cold, dark cell.

Through my darkness, Oryn blazed like the sun itself. I'd surrendered to his light, to the intoxicating feeling of being loved.

"And wait until you see your dress! It's fit for a goddess."

Guilt clawed at my insides.

I'd fallen in love with Oryn, truly and deeply. His kindness, his warmth, the way he looked at me like I hung the stars in the sky... it was everything I'd ever dreamed of. But was I betraying everything else I held dear by choosing this path?

You're choosing life, Maël's voice cut through my doubts. *You have a mate, Lor, blessed by the gods themselves. Would you risk their wrath by turning your back on such a gift?*

The mere thought of leaving Oryn, of shattering his heart, left me breathless with pain. I loved him. I craved this life with him. But my unfinished business loomed over me like a guillotine blade.

Maël's words echoed in my mind like a prayer. Mates were sacred, Oryn had told me, as rare as stars blazing across the sky. The window beckoned, promising freedom to continue my hunt for

Johan, but would the gods curse me for such defiance? Would I spend my life running, forever chasing shadows?

"Alora, are you alright?" Luella's concerned voice broke through my spiraling thoughts.

I forced a smile. "Yes, just... overwhelmed."

She squeezed my shoulder gently. "Everyone gets wedding nerves. But when you see Prince Oryn waiting for you, the world will right itself. Besides, you'll drive him mad looking this beautiful." Her laugh chimed like silver bells. She knew well how Oryn pursued me, from stolen moments in the library to every mundane escort through the palace halls.

I wanted to believe her promises of peace. Rising from the bath with Luella's help, I faced my reflection. A stranger stared back, caught between shadow and sunlight, belonging to neither.

She helped me into my wedding gown, the ivory silk flowed down my body, a lace covered corset accentuated my curves, with tiny gems sewn into the light material. Luella laced up the back, her enthusiasm bubbling over as she couldn't contain her joy as we both inspected the finished look. In her eyes, I could tell she saw a princess, one who treated her lady's maid as her equal, a romantic notion of a commoner turned royal.

I saw something else entirely, a fraud wearing silk and gems, a shadow masquerading as sunlight, a girl whose quest for revenge would forever stain her mate's golden name.

"Oh, Alora, you look absolutely breathtaking! Prince Oryn won't be able to take his eyes off you."

I forced a smile, grateful for her warmth, my fingers twisting in my lap to hide their trembling. As I sat at the vanity, Luella carefully pinned my hair, weaving in small white flowers that glowed like captured starlight against my dark strands, each bloom a delicate contrast between light and shadow.

"Oh, I almost forgot! A letter came in for you, my lady," she said, handing me an envelope.

I recognized Augustus' familiar scrawl immediately. Relief flooded through me as I read his words, he had departed early that morning, before dawn could paint the sky. I was thankful he'd be safe from whatever storm my choices might unleash, but his absence still left an ache in my chest.

As we prepared to leave for the ceremony, Magnus appeared at the door, striking in his formal uniform.

"You look radiant, Lady Alora," he said, his usual gruffness softened by genuine admiration.

We began our walk to the great hall, my nerves wreaking internal havoc with each step. Suddenly, I turned to Magnus.

"Magnus, would you... would you walk me down the aisle? Augustus won't be able to, and I—"

"It would be my honor, my lady," he replied, his voice thick with emotion.

With a grateful nod. Augustus's absence would raise few eyebrows. Most viewed him as a frail old man, and his poor health would provide a convenient excuse. Still, appearing without an escort would set the palace gossips aflame. Magnus was the next best choice.

We found Shefferd waiting at the grand hall's towering doors. His sweat dampened suit stretched tight across his frame as he directed the staff with frantic gestures.

"Excellent timing. We must proceed," he pressed a bouquet of golden flowers into my hands while hurrying Luella toward her next task. Magnus offered his arm and I took it, trying to hide my trembling.

"You'll make a fine princess, my lady," Magnus murmured as the ancient hinges groaned. "And one day, you'll be a great queen."

The moment we crossed the threshold, my gaze found Oryn. He stood resplendent at the altar, his golden hair blazing in the sunlight. His formal attire and gleaming medals transformed him from the casual prince I knew into every inch a royal heir. Our gazes locked, and heat surged through our bond, a sun bright tide of emotion.

Every step toward him, I felt the weight of our connection grow stronger. The bond thrummed between us like a living thing, each pulse sending shivers of golden warmth cascading through my veins, making my skin tingle as if touched by sunlight. By the time I reached the altar, the world beyond us dissolved into nothing but whispers. There was only us, our hands clasped together, our hearts beating as one.

This was the path I needed. To hell with every "what if" that plagued my mind before. I could have everything, my revenge against Johan, my mate, my future. No one would ever know. My heart twisted painfully in my chest, torn between the burning need for vengeance and the pure, golden love radiating through our bond. I could listen to Maël's voice in my head and just... just live. The thought settled in my chest like a prayer, a desperate hope that maybe, just maybe, I could find peace in Oryn's arms without sacrificing the justice my grandmother deserved.

Elvirana stood before us, her red and golden robes catching the light as she raised her hands to begin the ceremony. Her power brushed against my skin like static electricity, making the shadows within me curl and retreat from her probing magic.

"Today we join two hearts as one," she proclaimed, her voice echoing through the hall. "Our grand kingdom will rise with the power of this blessed union between these two souls." Her hands swept toward us in a grand gesture.

With each word, bile rose in my throat. They weren't celebrating love, they were celebrating power. Their desperate hope that I would somehow amplify their precious sun magic made my skin crawl.

Terror clawed at my chest.

Elvirana's voice faded to a distant hum as darkness crept into the edges of my vision. My hands trembled in Oryn's warm grip like autumn leaves in a storm.

He squeezed them gently, sending waves of golden warmth through our bond. His eyes captured mine, brimming with such pure love and promise that my heart splintered beneath the weight of my deception.

"The ancient laws of our people dictate that true mates are blessed by the gods themselves," Elvirana continued, her gnarled fingers weaving through the air.

"Such a union not only strengthens the mates but weaves power into the very foundation of our realm. May the gods shine their favor upon this bond."

I tensed at her words about power, acutely aware of the shadows coiled beneath my skin and the dormant fire that could reduce this pristine palace to cinders.

The urge to flee surged through me, to melt into the shadows where monsters like me belonged.

But Oryn's thumb traced gentle patterns on my palm, his presence in my mind wrapping around me like a warm embrace.

The mate bond sang between us, pure and perfect, pulling me closer until the rest of the world blurred at the edges.

"The joining of two suns," Elvirana declared, each word a blade against my conscience. "A union foretold by time itself..."

Stay strong, little hunter, Maël's voice whispered through my mind. *You deserve happiness. You deserve your mate.*

I desperately wanted to believe him, to embrace this love, this chance at belonging. But Johan's face invaded my thoughts, followed by the echo of screams and the memory of my grandmother's last breath.

Through our bond, Oryn sensed my distress, his grip tightening on my hands.

I gazed into his cerulean eyes, finding warmth and acceptance that made my heart ache.

He stood before me, ready to bind his life to mine, blind to the darkness I harbored. To the blood on my hands. To the vengeance that burned in my soul.

The ceremony flowed around us like water while my conscience waged war within.

My heart yearned to choose this path with him, but the shadows whispered their cruel truth. How could I be both his radiant princess and Death's Wraith? His beloved wife and the blade in the dark?

Elvirana guided us through the traditional vows, her voice echoing through the vast chamber.

Oryn's hands cradled mine like precious treasures as he spoke, each word a golden chain binding my heart to his.

"I vow to cherish you, to protect you, to stand beside you through whatever storms may come. You are my heart, my home, my mate. From this day until my last."

The crowd fell silent, breathless at his declaration. Their beloved prince had found his true mate.

A sacred bond meant to last eternally. One that wrapped around my throat like a noose of guilt.

Our bond throbbed between us like a second heartbeat, growing stronger with each passing moment.

Golden threads of light seemed to weave around our joined hands, dancing like living fire in the sunlight streaming through the windows.

When my turn came, the words spilled from my lips like water from a spring, surprising even me.

"I vow to be your shelter in darkness, your companion in light. To face whatever comes at your side, to share in your joys and sorrows. From this day until my last."

Our bond ignited like wildfire, burning away my doubts in its golden blaze. Oryn's joy crashed over me like waves, his love pouring through our connection until I could barely breathe from its intensity.

"By the ancient power of sun and stars," Elvirana declared, her voice resonating through the hall, "I now pronounce you bound as one, prince and princess of Sunneva."

Oryn's fingers brushed my cheek like sunlight breaking through storm clouds. When his lips claimed mine, liquid fire coursed through my veins, igniting every nerve ending.

The mate bond exploded between us, a supernova of golden light and raw power that consumed everything else.

Reality narrowed to this single point in time, the taste of his kiss, his thoughts weaving through mine like threads of sunlight through shadow, our hearts finding their shared rhythm.

When we parted, his radiant smile outshone every star in the heavens.

His euphoria flooded our bond, a tidal wave of pure, golden love that threatened to drown my darkness.

The assembled court burst into celebration, their voices distant and hollow compared to the symphony of Oryn's joy singing through our bond and the guilty drumming of my heart.

CHAPTER 35

I was lost in a hazy dream when I felt a tender touch on my cheek, warm and intimate like the first rays of dawn. The warmth of his touch sent tingles across my skin, his scent—citrus and sandalwood—wrapped around me like a cherished memory. Slowly, I blinked my eyes open, the world blurring at its edges like watercolors in rain. Oryn's face came into focus, his golden hair catching the light like molten metal. The morning after our wedding dawned with a sweetness I never thought possible. The moment felt as fragile as frost on glass, as precious as the last star before dawn.

"Lor," he whispered, his voice ghosting across my skin. "I'm sorry to wake you, Love."

I murmured nonsense, fighting against the fog of dreams that clung to my mind. Oryn's thumb traced my jawline, and I melted into his touch. The vulnerability of the moment twisted something painful in my chest.

"I have to leave for a few days," he continued, his words drifting through my sleep-addled mind. "There's something I need to check at the war front." Dread coiled in my chest, even through the haze of sleep.

"War front?" I muttered, my brow furrowing slightly. Fear sparked in my thoughts, but sleep held me prisoner.

Oryn leaned down, pressing a lingering kiss to my forehead. "Sleep, my love. I'll return soon enough."

I felt his lips brush against mine, warm and inviting. I returned the kiss lazily, already drifting back towards slumber.

"Be safe," I managed to murmur as my eyes fluttered closed.

The last thing I registered was his silent retreat as Oryn moved away from the bed, taking his warmth with him. Then, sleep claimed me once more, pulling me back into its dark embrace. A voice in my dreams whispered that this farewell carried the weight of finality.

I JOLTED AWAKE, my heart racing. The room was dark as a starless night, save for a sliver of moonlight peeking through the heavy curtains. Disoriented, I reached out, searching for Oryn's familiar warmth. My hand met cold sheets instead.

Reality slammed into me like a tidal wave. Oryn was gone, off to the war front. I was alone, the emptiness of his absence a hollow ache in my chest.

Sighing, I pushed myself up and fumbled for the lamp on my bedside table. The soft glow illuminated my chambers, casting long shadows across the bookshelves that surrounded me like silent guardians. My sanctuary, now feeling more like a prison of memories.

Unable to shake the unease that wrapped around me like a shroud, I slipped out of bed and padded across the room. I trailed my fingers along the spines of my beloved books, drawing comfort from their course textures.

The night felt dead silent. No chirping crickets, no rustling leaves. Nothing but the weight of emptiness.

A whisper ghosted past my ears, so faint I thought I'd imagined it. I froze, straining to listen.

A sound sharp as a blade sliding through silk. Coming from outside my window. Through the moonlit glass, shadows danced across the castle grounds, too fluid to be natural. My eyes darted towards a leather tome on the shelf beside me where I had hidden a dagger just in case. Ice flooded my veins as another whisper slithered through the air, raising the fine hairs on my neck.

Before I could move, the window shattered in a spray of deadly shards. Figures cloaked in darkness slipped through the broken window, their faces nothing more than bottomless voids. I opened my mouth to scream, but a leather clad hand clamped over it, silencing my terror.

Iron like grips seized my arms, crushing them against my body. Before I could call my shadows for help, I felt a sharp pinch in my neck. I fought wildly, kicking out, but my bare feet found only emptiness. My legs lost their strength, everything began to blur. My muddled mind fought to stay coherent, to remember what's happening so I could get away. The intruders lifted me up like I weighed nothing, carrying me towards the broken window. The room spun like a twisted carousel, my vision darkening at the edges as whatever poison they'd used spread through my blood like liquid frost.

The shadows in my room writhed and twisted, responding to my panic even as my power slipped away. They reached for me with desperate fingers of darkness, but without my conscious control, they could only watch helplessly as I was taken.

Dark figures dragged my limp body through the shattered window into the bitter night air. My arms hung uselessly at my sides, my head lolling back as my muscles refused to obey. Could Oryn sense my terror through our mate bond, or had these creatures waited for the precise moment when our connection was weakest? The usual hum of our golden thread was deafeningly silent, like a snuffed-out star. They must have planned this, watching and waiting for the perfect moment when I was most vulnerable.

Panic clawed at my throat, trapped behind my captor's iron grip. My lungs burned for air, each shallow breath a battle against the leather-clad fingers crushing against my mouth.

Terror froze my blood. Our closed bond meant Oryn might never know what happened. He could return to find nothing but broken glass and my abandoned books, with no way to track where they'd taken me.

The poison spread deeper through my veins as they carried me into darkness. My last conscious thought was of golden hair and citrus-scented warmth, now impossibly far away. Then everything went black.

CHAPTER 36

The world spun as I woke on a cold stone floor. I groaned, my body aching from the struggle. As my eyes adjusted to the gloom, the reality of my situation sank in.

The plush furnishings and warmth of my chambers had vanished. In their place, damp stone walls pressed closer with each breath, the air heavy with rot and decay.

I pushed myself up, hissing as the icy stone bit into my bare feet. The cold seeped through my skin, straight into my bones, making my teeth chatter uncontrollably. Chains rattled, and I realized with horror that my ankles were shackled, the iron heavy and unyielding against my skin. Just days ago, I'd lounged in silks surrounded by my beloved books, losing myself in tales of adventure and romance without a care in the world. Now fate had thrown me into this hellish place, and those peaceful moments felt like nothing more than a distant dream. I huddled against the wall, my thin nightgown offering no protection from the bone deep chill, and wrapped my arms around myself in a futile attempt to preserve what little warmth remained. The damp fabric clung to my skin like a second layer of ice, each breath visible in the frigid air.

Desperately, I reached for the familiar tendrils of shadow that usually came so easily to my call, but they slipped through my grasp like smoke. Whether from exhaustion or something more sinister, my power remained frustratingly out of reach. My chest tightened with panic as I clawed at that dark well inside me where my magic usually resided, finding nothing but hollow emptiness. The shadows that had always been my faithful companions, my weapons, my shields, now abandoned me when I needed them most. Each failed attempt left me more drained than the last, like trying to draw water from a dried up well with nothing but a broken bucket.

"Welcome to the royal dungeons," a rough voice echoed from the darkness.

I spun toward the sound, my heart thundering against my ribs. From the shadows emerged a man, his matted beard streaked with filth, his eyes burning with an unsettling gleam. His tattered prison clothes hung from his muscular frame like moth-eaten curtains, and the stench of unwashed flesh and the filth of the cells made my nose wrinkle. There was something not entirely right about him, something that made my instincts scream danger even without my shadows to warn me. Perhaps it was the way he moved, too fluid for someone who looked so decrepit, or how those fever bright eyes seemed to see straight through my carefully constructed walls.

"Who are you?" I demanded, forcing steel into my voice despite my fear.

A broken laugh rasped from his throat. "Just another forgotten soul in these depths. Though I suppose misery craves company."

His presence brought no comfort, only more questions that clawed at my mind. "Why are we here? Who imprisoned us?"

Something sinister crossed the man's features. "Who do you think? The sun blessed royals of Sunneva. After all, this is their dungeon." He scoffed as if it were a waste of his time to even answer. "Don't you like what they've done to the place?"

Ice flooded my veins. "What do you mean? Prince Oryn would never allow me to be brought here."

He shuffled closer, narrowed eyes almost softening with pity. "Don't be so sure. No one is brought here by accident."

"No," the word tore from my throat as I backed away. "You're wrong about him. Oryn wouldn't—" My fingers curled into fists, nails biting crescents into my palms as bile rose in my throat.

Royals care only for their crowns. They'll crush anyone beneath their boots to keep their precious power.

Chains rattled as he dragged himself closer to the bars separating us. "They call me Rasher."

His words coiled around my mind like poison-tipped thorns, tainting every tender memory we'd created. I could barely whisper my name through numb lips as I pressed myself against the frigid wall, willing the stones to swallow me whole. Anything to escape the crushing weight of betrayal that threatened to shatter my chest.

The Oryn who had stolen my heart with soft caresses and earnest smiles that tasted of sunlight and citrus promises couldn't have betrayed me.

Yet doubt slithered through my mind like frost across glass, crystallizing into dark patterns across every shared smile, every whispered secret between us.

The mate bond in my chest ached, a hollow reminder of what we'd shared, or what I'd foolishly believed we'd shared.

I'd danced with death and played with fire, surviving against impossible odds.

But in this wretched pit, with betrayal burning like acid on my tongue, the walls of my resolve began to splinter.

If my golden prince had truly betrayed me, what hope remained in this darkness? My chest constricted as if bound by iron bands, each breath a battle against the weight of his betrayal. Shadows danced at the edges of my vision, mocking my powerlessness, I who commanded darkness now drowning in it. The cruel irony wasn't lost on me that his sunlight, which once warmed my cold heart, now threatened to burn everything we'd built to ash.

CHAPTER 37

The iron-bound door to my cell creaked open with an ominous groan that set my teeth on edge, and rough, calloused hands jerked me to my feet. I stumbled, my legs trembling and weak from days of confinement in this goddess-cursed dungeon. They dragged me down a dimly lit corridor, my heart pounding with each footfall echoing against cold stone. The torchlight cast dancing shadows on the damp walls, and I fought to keep my breathing steady as fear threatened to choke me. My captors' grip branded bruises into my skin, but I refused to give them the satisfaction of hearing me whimper.

We entered a cavernous room, the ceiling vanishing into darkness overhead. The space was dominated by a figure shrouded in shadows, their form a wraith-like silhouette against the far wall. As they shoved me forward, my bare feet catching on jagged stone, I caught a glimpse of gleaming instruments on nearby tables, metal that glinted wickedly in the torchlight like a predator's smile. My stomach churned, bile rising in my throat as I recognized implements whose only purpose was to torture.

"Well, well... if it isn't the famed princess," a silky voice slithered from the darkness, each word dripping with poisoned honey that made my skin crawl. "I've been waiting so long for this moment."

Their voice carried an accent as old as the forgotten kingdoms, refined yet corrupted, like something beautiful left to rot.

Drawing on what little strength remained, I forced steel into my voice despite the terror flooding my veins. "Who are you? What could you possibly want?" The words burned like cinders on my tongue.

The figure glided into the torchlight, revealing features carved by cruel curiosity. Those predatory eyes cut through me like knives, calculating and cold. Their lips twisted into something that might have passed for a smile on another face, but here it promised only agony. Dark skin inked with a glittering substance glinted in the light, jagged swirls framed their face and flowed down their neck disappearing beneath their coat. "Your magic calls to me. Such extraordinary power. I must know every secret it holds." Their fingers danced across the gleaming instruments with terrible tenderness.

Fear clawed at my throat as they strapped me to an ice-cold metal table, its surface slick with condensation. The restraints bit into my wrists and ankles with brutal efficiency. I reached deep within myself, desperately trying to call forth my shadows, that familiar darkness that had always come when I needed it most. Nothing happened. The emptiness where my power should have been gaped like an open wound in my chest, and panic bloomed fresh and sharp in its place.

"Ah, ah," the figure tsked, lips curling into a serpentine smile. Their voice dripped with honeyed venom that sent shivers down my spine. They held up a vial of shimmering liquid, turning it this way and that so the contents caught the harsh light above. Rainbow like tendrils writhed within the glass, hypnotic and deadly. "A little concoction to keep your powers at bay. Fascinating how it works, really. The way it binds to your very essence, like a lock without a key."

Terror clawed up my throat, a living thing that threatened to burst through my ribs as they began their twisted experiments. Each probe, each precise incision carved away pieces of my soul, as if they were trying to peel back layers of my soul along with my flesh. I thrashed against my restraints until hot blood traced burning trails down my wrists, the metallic scent of blood mixing with antiseptic and fear.

"Stop!" I screamed. The word ripped from my throat like shattered glass, tears carving burning trails down my temples into my hair. "Please!" Defeat tasted like bitter ash on my tongue.

My pleas echoed uselessly against stone walls. As agony clawed deeper into my flesh, my mind fractured, desperately seeking escape in buried memories. My screams faded to nothing.

Reality splintered like broken mirror shards, each piece reflecting fragments of a past I'd fought to bury.

Through the fog of torment, a voice pierced the darkness. Familiar. Impossible. My name, whispered in tones I knew better than my own heartbeat. The sound brushed against my mind like a gentle touch, a lifeline in an ocean of pain.

The comfort vanished like smoke between my fingers as fresh agony ripped through me, pulling me under.

In a heartbeat, I was young again, racing through woods where sunlight danced between leaves. Maël's laughter rang pure and bright around me as we chased each other toward our sanctuary. The ancient oak reached for us with gnarled branches, its trunk scarred with years of our climbing. Wild honeysuckle and fresh moss filled my nose, a memory so vivid it made my heart ache.

"Come on, Lor!" he called, his fingers finding each familiar handhold with practiced ease as he scaled the trunk. "I bet you can't catch me!" Sunlight filtered through the leaves, turning his brown hair to molten gold.

A grin spread across my face as I accepted his challenge, my small hands finding purchase on the rough bark. We would spend hours in that tree, our legs dangling from the highest branches we dared climb, whispering our dreams and fears into the wind. The future stretched before us like an endless road we thought we'd walk together.

The memory rippled and changed, pulling me to the training grounds years later. Maël's brown eyes sparked with mischief as he feinted left, catching me off guard. Morning light caught the sweat on his skin, turning each droplet into liquid gold.

"You're getting slow, little hunter," he taunted, flashing that crooked smile that never failed to make my heart stumble in its rhythm.

I lunged forward, my dagger finding its mark into his leather vest. "Not slow enough for you," I shot back, both of us smirking. Our bodies moved in perfect sync, close enough that I could feel the heat radiating from his skin, smell the woodsy scent that was uniquely Maël. The clash of steel against steel sang around us, a deadly dance we'd perfected over years of shared history.

The memory shattered, dissolving like morning mist. My stomach lurched as the past rearranged itself, the warmth of that training session violently replaced by the grandeur of my wedding day. The great hall of the Sun Palace glittered beneath thousands of crystals, each one catching and fracturing light into kaleidoscope patterns. I remembered how my heart had thundered when I saw Oryn waiting for me at the end of that sea of faces, his golden hair crowned by actual sunlight streaming through the stained glass windows, his ceremonial whites making him look like a god descended from the heavens.

His smile lit up the hall as he claimed my hands in his. "My mate," he breathed, those light eyes filled with a promise I foolishly believed. In that moment, our bond had hummed between us like a living thing, filling my chest with golden warmth and the taste of citrus on my tongue. Now, the memory of his touch carved new wounds into my chest, more brutal than any torture. How quickly that golden prince had turned to shadow, leaving nothing but ashes where our love had burned.

My body trembled on the cold metal table, tears mixing with blood as the memories threatened to break me completely.

Like a twisted game of the gods, they had given me perfect happiness before snatching it away.

His betrayal pressed against my lungs like a stone, stealing my breath.

Every heartbeat drove invisible blades deeper between my ribs.

Bound to this frozen table, I suffered while my husband, my mate, stood with my tormentors.

Where his presence once burned bright in my mind, our bond now lay cold and empty.

Were the gentle touches lies? The soft promises false? Had he ever truly seen me as his everything?

Warm blood traced patterns down my arm where metal bit into skin.

The cuts and bruises meant nothing against the raw wound in my soul.

This dungeon would become my tomb, my body left to their cruel curiosity.

Maël wouldn't come, lost in the years between us. Oryn wouldn't come, his love nothing but deceit.

Black mist crawled across my sight as their poison spread through my veins.

I embraced the darkness, praying for endless sleep. Oblivion seemed kinder than living with his betrayal.

CHAPTER 38

Time blurred into a meaningless haze.

Consciousness returned only to find me in one of two places: the damp cell or the cold table.

My only markers of time became the irregular deliveries of stale water and moldy gruel, and when Rasher offered his sparse conversation.

His accent and bitter words about the royal family marked him as no Sunnevan.

The cold edge to his voice betrayed his Esmeray origins.

Sometimes I found the provisions waiting. More often, drugged stupor clouded my mind during their visits.

A hooded figure brought the rations, their form obscured by heavy black robes, hands hidden beneath thick gloves.

The food and water carried a bitter undertone, and darkness claimed me soon after each meal.

Pride kept me from eating until hunger broke my resolve.

Without sustenance, I'd never find the strength to escape.

Vanya's training had covered torture and capture, but nothing could have prepared me for this systematic destruction.

What would she think of her heir now, trapped and broken?

Though lips remained sealed, my secrets locked away, I could still feel myself losing in this dark game.

Better to die with honor than break under torture. If they gave me a blade, I'd end this nightmare myself.

I've learned my tormentor calls themself the Alchemist. Each session leaves another cut carved into my flesh. The cuts were precise. Clinical. Just deep enough to draw blood for whatever twisted purpose they had in mind. Sometimes consciousness breaks through their potions. In those moments, their ravings about blood magic and gods echo through my drugged haze.

This time, they wanted me awake for their experiments. Cold metal restraints bit into my wrists and ankles. The chain around my throat allowed barely enough room to breathe.

The Alchemist loomed over me, dark satisfaction glinting in their eyes. "Your beloved prince seems in no hurry to find you."

I attempted to jerk my head aside as much as the chain allows, but their words found their mark like poisoned arrows.

"Oh, come now. Surely you've wondered why no one's come for you?" The Alchemist's poisoned words slithered against my skin as they leaned closer to my ear. "After all, your dear prince has been quite occupied. Word is he's already selected a new bride to replace his vanished princess." My muscles tensed beneath the restraints, a slight tremor running through my limbs despite my efforts to remain still.

"You're lying," I snarled, but doubt clawed at my heart.

They produced a scroll, letting it cascade open before my eyes. "See for yourself."

My eyes raked across the parchment, my heart plummeting as I recognized the kingdom's gossip column. There were no demands for my whereabouts, only stories of Oryn and...Ingrid and the idea that she would be taking my place and healing my poor lonely mate's heart. My fingers trembled against the cold metal restraints, nausea coiling in my gut.

"He never truly loved you, you know," their poisoned words slithered through my mind. "He saw the power you hold and sent you to me. To harness such an important gift."

The sight of Ingrid's name made bile rise in my throat. I squeezed my eyes shut, willing the text away. Tears burned behind my closed lids as memories of our wedding night crashed through my defenses. The tenderness in Oryn's gaze, the warmth of his touch. Had it all been nothing but a beautiful lie?

"Please," I whispered, the word breaking as my resolve shattered.

"Face the truth, Alora. You're alone. Abandoned. Forgotten." The Alchemist's dark laughter echoed through the chamber as they mixed my blood with something that glowed an unnatural blue, their quill scratching frantically across parchment.

"While the Artans possess great power, their blood lacks a certain... essence." Glass clinked against metal as they moved between their vials and instruments.

"But yours..." A glass shattered against stone. "Your blood contains exactly what I need."

"Perhaps the bloodlines must be... merged." Their words sent ice through my veins.

"We'll make her ascend one way or another," they whispered reverently. "All the power of the gods flowing through her veins."

Their dark muttering grew closer as they approached, brandishing another needle that caught the torchlight.

"Touch me, and I'll ensure you all suffer," I snarled, thrashing against the chains while they loomed above me, lips twisted in a cruel smile.

"Oh little pet, you won't live long enough to try."

The needle pierced my skin like a shard of ice, and liquid fire spread through my veins.

"You're the key I've been waiting for." Their words blurred at the edges as darkness crept into my vision, the potion dragging me down into another imprisoning slumber.

MY CAPTORS' words echoed through my mind, wearing away at my hope like water on stone. I began to question everything—my memories, my feelings, even my own worth. Each taunt, each cruel reminder of my isolation carved deeper wounds than their physical torments ever could.

In the rare moments of solitude, I'd stare at my hands, willing my shadows to appear. But the magic that had once been an integral part of me remained frustratingly out of reach, like trying to grasp smoke. The emptiness where that power used to reside felt like a hollow cavity in my chest, another reminder of everything I'd lost.

"What's the point?" I murmured to the cold cell, my voice cracking.

"Pardon?" Rasher's deep voice drifted through the silence.

My stomach churned with acid recalling the document my captor had shown me—the one detailing Ryn and Ingrid's involvement, my throat closing with each strangled breath. The memory of his citrus and sandalwood scent turned acrid in my mind, a mockery of everything we'd shared.

The thought of her triumph sent rage coursing through my veins like poison. My nails carved bloody half-moons into my palms as her mocking laughter haunted my thoughts, a phantom sound that refused to fade.

Weariness crushed me beneath its weight, turning my limbs to lead and each breath into a battle.

Freedom became a cruel mirage, shimmering just beyond reach, mocking me with promises it would never keep.

No doubt she was reveling in her victory, celebrating my imprisonment while she claimed what was mine. What should have been mine.

Drawing my knees to my chest, I pressed against the stone wall and gazed at my only ally in this wretched prison.

"What was the point of any of this? The marriage. The mate bond." My voice cracked with bitterness. "If they only wanted to use me, to claim my body, why bother with the charade?"

Nothing made sense anymore.

"They'll tear you apart and leave nothing but scraps," Rasher said, his shadow stark against the iron bars.

"Keep your wits sharp. While there's breath in your lungs, there's fight left in your soul."

I huddled against the frigid stone, a broken thing seeking comfort where none existed. Reality pressed against my closed eyelids, refusing to grant even the mercy of temporary escape.

In that moment, surrender whispered through my mind like a poisoned caress.

The shadows that once answered my call now pressed against me like a shroud, suffocating and cruel. They whispered of failure and loss, of hopes crumbling to dust on my tongue.

CHAPTER 39

I lay there, broken and defeated, when a familiar voice echoed in my mind. Maël's voice, from so long ago.

Get up, little hunter. The fight's not over yet.

My eyes snapped open.

Memories crashed through me like a tidal wave—Maël, the village, Grandmother. Every face I'd lost kindled something fierce in my soul.

"No," I whispered, pushing myself up. Survival blazed through my veins like wildfire.

My legs shook as I rose. The cell tilted and spun, but I locked my jaw and forced the world to steady.

"I still have debts to collect."

The shadows writhed in the corners, answering my call. I stretched out my hand, welcoming the icy kiss of my magic as the suppressant's chains began to crack.

Burn them all, Lor.

Maël, I breathed, relief washing through me at his voice. *I didn't know true lunacy until I could only hear my own thoughts.*

You're stuck with me, Lor, but you need to go. Now.

Chaos exploded beyond my cell. Metal screamed against metal, voices raised in alarm.

Through our bond, Oryn's presence battered against my mental walls like a storm. But I reinforced them, and they would hold.

The door crashed inward. The Alchemist stormed in, panic twisting his glittering features.

"You wretched girl!" he snarled, lunging for me.

But I wasn't his prisoner anymore.

Darkness wrapped around my fist like a lover's caress. I struck true, my knuckles crushing into his face. The alchemist reeled backward.

Blood streamed between his fingers as he clutched his face. "The suppressants," he choked out. "You shouldn't have any power!"

I stalked forward, shadows swirling around me. Every step fed my rage. The endless torture. The bitter betrayal. The cruel violations. My fists curled as heat surged through me. I glanced down to find my white flames licking my hands. Darkness coiled around the brilliant flames like serpents, casting an otherworldly radiance. This kingdom would burn for what they'd done. I would purge this land of its corruption. Starting with this monster before me.

The Alchemist stumbled away, fleeing through the open door.

A ring of keys glinted on a fallen guard's belt. I snatched them up, flinging them toward Rasher's waiting hands.

Freedom blazed in his desperate eyes.

"Wait!" Rasher's plea echoed behind me, but I was already charging through the dungeon door. Vengeance consumed me, leaving no room for allies or aid. The Alchemist was mine to destroy.

Rage fueled my pursuit as I hunted the coward through the shadowed hallway. Guards charged to intercept me, but my fury made quick work of them. Tendrils of shadow whipped through the air, binding their limbs while fire blazed across my hands. They dropped like stones, writhing as my dual powers consumed them.

His terrified screams beckoned me forward like a siren's call. He would answer for each moment of torment. For every violation of body and mind. For trying to break my spirit.

I crashed through the doors of his laboratory, toxic fumes burning my nose and throat.

Glass containers covered every surface, each holding evidence of his perverse research. My gaze swept around, hunting for my prey.

The Alchemist burst from his hiding place behind a door, brandishing a syringe in his shaking grip. Before I could move, he drove the needle into my neck. Liquid fire coursed through my veins as his poison spread.

The shadows retreated, my flames guttered, both powers dimming like stars at dawn. His cruel laughter echoed through the room as reality tilted and blurred.

"Did you truly believe you could break free?" His glittering face twisted with malicious delight. His dark features contorted with a sadistic pleasure that made my skin crawl. "I will strip away every spark of power you possess. Death will become your dearest wish."

His dark promises followed me into the growing void. But I refused to surrender to the darkness. Blood welled beneath my nails as I clenched my fists, fighting the poison's pull with every heartbeat. My vision swam, but I forced myself to remain standing, even as my legs threatened to give way beneath me.

A bone-chilling shriek sliced through the haze, more terrifying than anything I'd ever known.

The Alchemist's screams ripped through the laboratory, raw terror bleeding into each desperate sound.

My legs gave out beneath me, but not before I saw something shift in the doorway. A towering shadow stood there, backlit by dancing flames.

The shadow glided forward with lethal grace, and an unexpected peace settled over my racing heart. Death had come for his wraith at last, and I greeted him like an old friend.

Darkness beckoned with open arms, and I surrendered to its pull as reality slipped through my fingers. The alchemist's tortured screams faded into the distance like leaves scattered by an autumn breeze.

Until nothing remained but blessed silence.

Acknowledgments

Whew! It's felt like a lifetime of developing and writing the beginning of Alora's journey. I always dreamed of writing a book...and now I've signed on for three! Daughter of Shadows and Ash has prevailed against what has probably been the craziest year of my life. There were several times where I didn't think I would ever get this finished, but this goes to show how important it is to build your community. Mine helped keep me motivated to get here.

I wanted to thank the amazing artists who helped bring the pages to life: INK Designs, Paige Annabentleah, and Lourdes Navarrete. Especially for knowing "the thing" when I myself wasn't exactly sure.

Thank you to my ARC readers, you have no idea how grateful I am to have you take a chance on me and I hope you enjoyed Daughter of Shadows and Ash as much as I enjoyed writing it.

To my friends and family, thank you for putting up with me while I holed myself up to finish this. I wouldn't have been able to finish this without you. Sam, I cannot begin to describe how much your unwavering support has carried me through this journey. Thank you for humoring me with discussions and for always lifting me up.

Also by Ember Johnson

<u>Araceli's Blade Trilogy</u>

Daughter of Shadows and Ash

Princess of Flames and Fate

Queen of Stars and Wrath

<u>Best Fangs Forever</u>

Blind Bite

Ember Johnson writes tales steeped in starlight and shadows. Her books will take you to new realms filled with whimsical settings, strong heroines, wicked banter, and book boyfriends that bite.

You'll often find her curled up on her couch with a hot cup of tea writing an unhinged plot line for the lore or reading her new favorite fantasy romance. There's an 80% chance it's a reverse harem/why choose, fantasy romance in a dark academic setting.

Ember cohabitates with her husband who has still to this day not finished reading her debut. His qualm is that she "killed him" as his favorite character died. Unfortunately, no characters are safe in any series. Together they survive the daily chaotic antics of their two children, dog, and cat.

instagram.com/author.emberjohnson

tiktok.com/@author.emberjohnson

threads.com/@author.emberjohnson

reamstories.com/emberjohnson

goodreads.com/emberjohnson